Praise for *Tom Trueheart*

'a pleasure to hold, read aloud and explore' **The Times**

Beck's prose has a crisp and springy rhythm - a treat to read
d to anyone over the age of six. His illustrations, gnarled silhou-
s, are marvellously complex. If you turn them upside down,
change completely. A volume to treasure.' **The Telegraph**

elightful book, and one with a wide potential audience . . . a
y with a timeless quality and great charm for bedtime reading
ards.' **The Literary Review**

ks likely to become one of the hits of 2006 . . . It is all rollocking,
bustious stuff, with plenty of jokes' **The Times**

" handsome little book with striking silhouette illustrations,
c ains a wonderful story.' **lovereadingforkids.com**

" m's quest to discover his own story and his courage unrolls
t ough an elegantly described magical landscape, in this skilful,
highly inventive story about the way stories work.' **Booktrust**

'*Tom Trueheart* is beautifully put together. The illustrations, the
layout, even the size and feel of the book are extraordinarily
pleasing . . . This is a fast, easy read for children who are comfortable with longer chapter books.' **Writeaway**

THE VALE of WOODCUTTERS

THE DARK CASTLE

THE LAND of DARK STORIES

OXFORD
UNIVERSITY PRESS

Great Clarendon Street, Oxford OX2 6DP

Oxford University Press is a department of the University of Oxford.
It furthers the University's objective of excellence in research, scholarship,
and education by publishing worldwide in

Oxford New York

Auckland Cape Town Dar es Salaam Hong Kong Karachi
Kuala Lumpur Madrid Melbourne Mexico City Nairobi
New Delhi Shanghai Taipei Toronto

With offices in

Argentina Austria Brazil Chile Czech Republic France Greece
Guatemala Hungary Italy Japan Poland Portugal Singapore
South Korea Switzerland Thailand Turkey Ukraine Vietnam

Oxford is a registered trade mark of Oxford University Press
in the UK and in certain other countries

British Library Cataloguing in Publication Data
Data available

ISBN: 978-0-19-279213-6

1 3 5 7 9 10 8 6 4 2

Printed in Great Britain by CPI Cox and Wyman, Reading, RG1 8EX

Paper used in the production of this book is a natural,
recyclable product made from wood grown in sustainable forests.
The manufacturing process conforms to the environmental
regulations of the country of origin.

www.tomtrueheart.com

TOM TRUEHEART
and the Land of Dark Stories

IAN BECK

OXFORD
UNIVERSITY PRESS

Part One
An Unhappy Ending

Chapter 1

Once upon a time there was a family of adventurers called the Truehearts, and their neat wooden house sat near a crossroads, not far from the Land of Stories. The house was painted in bright contrasting colours: red and green. The timber walls were painted red, and the shutters, with their heart-shaped cut-out holes, were painted green. On the roof there was a chimney stack and an iron chimney pipe which was topped with a wind cowl and a weathervane. The weathervane was made of iron, forged in the shape of a witch riding on a broomstick with her familiar cat, a recent gift from the Master of the Story Bureau

3

himself. Early on a perfect midsummer morning, a big black crow landed on top of the weathervane. The bird settled itself, fluffed up its feathers and waited . . .

Inside the cosy house, the youngest of the family, Tom Trueheart, was already having a horrible morning. Something dreadful was due to happen to him, and Tom could not see any way of getting out of it. Should he just stay in bed for a little while longer and try to escape by staying very quiet and hiding, or should he open his bedroom window, slide down the roof, hop into the garden, shimmy over the fence, and be away on an adventure, with (hopefully) his old friend Jollity the crow, before anyone noticed that he had gone at all?

He would have liked to enjoy this particular day-dream, but there was so much noise outside his little attic bedroom, such a crashing on the stairs, such a clat-tering of wood against wood, that it was hard for him to even think straight, let alone try and organize a running-away attempt. It was, of course, two of his older brothers jousting with quarterstaffs on the stairs.

The noise outside his door got steadily worse and the moment of decision would soon come. He knew that he should get up, brace himself, and help his mother with the breakfast. He knew that he would soon have to get ready, just like all his big beefy brothers, for the

EVENT.

There was a sudden huge crash, followed by more blistering cracks of wood against wood, followed by the stomping of big feet in big boots, and then by gales of raucous laughter. Tom decided, reluctantly, glumly, that perhaps it really was time to get up and face . . . IT.

IT was the terror from the dark place . . .

IT was the horror from beyond the woods . . .

IT was the thing on the hanger downstairs . . .

IT was . . . a white silk velvet pageboy suit, with a lace collar, ribbon bow, satin knee breeches, and high lace-up kid leather boots! For today was the big day. For most of Tom's big, bold, brave, and beefy brothers, it was their wedding day!

For Tom, it was set to be utter humiliation, for he was to be the pageboy, just as his mother had threatened all those months ago last winter. The wedding was meant to have taken place in the spring, but the Master had suggested waiting until the summer roses were in full bloom at the Story Bureau. And so it was: midsummer morning and it was all about to happen.

There was another series of escalating thumps from outside his door. Putting things off for just a moment longer, Tom hopped out of bed and went and looked out of the heart-shaped holes in the wooden shutters across his window.

'*Please* let there be a hurricane, or a freak storm. *Please* let a rogue sprite set off a sudden blizzard of ice and snow,' he said aloud to himself.

But no, when he looked out he could see that it was as perfect a summer morning as any princess bride and her bold adventurer bridegroom could wish for. Fluffy white clouds sailed across a celestial blue sky, while somewhere nearby a blackbird sang his liquid song.

'Oh no,' Tom said, 'it's lovely.' The weather certainly wasn't going to be of any help to him today, there would be no escape.

Later, after a typically noisy and chaotic breakfast, Tom washed up the bowls at the sink. Jack sat near him on the window seat. 'That's not proper work for a boy, is it. You're coddling him, our mother; he needs to keep on with some more real hard training, and soon, at that.'

'Don't you mind about our Tom,' said his mother, and she gave Tom a squeeze. 'You sometimes do your best to make him feel small; you leave him be. Tom is doing just fine, he'll be good and ready soon enough. Don't forget, the old hermit taught him all his letters and numbers many summers ago now, and lately our Jake's been teaching him his forest craft, and he will be carrying on his adventure training with you for the rest of the summer, so there's really no need to bully him now, is there.'

After washing up the breakfast things Tom went outside. He picked up a good sized twig, and waved it about as if it were his sword. Then he found a huge spider's web glistening in the early morning sun. He poked at the web with the twig, and watched the spider as it came running down the filament. It had a fat pale body and hairy little legs. Jack always said that some spiders had poison sacs and they could give you a nasty nip if you weren't careful. Then he whacked a crab apple with the twig and then he kicked another crab apple and chased after it across the bright grass and around to the front of the house; anything to put off the dreaded moment and THE SUIT.

Chapter 2

Tom stood for a while in the warm sunshine dreaming of an escape. By rights he ought to be off on a new adventure with his old friend Jollity the crow. Oh, how he hoped that might happen, and it couldn't happen soon enough. Jollity had promised all those months ago that he would come and rescue him from being the pageboy, but so far there was not a sign of him. It was then that he heard the welcome 'caw, caw' sound of a crow, and when he looked up at the weathervane, his spirits lifted, for a large crow sat there quietly waiting, and watching him.

'Oh, so there you are,' Tom said. 'Thank goodness, at last.'

At that moment the front door banged open, and Jake stomped out in his best big seven-league boots.

The startled crow flew up and off and away.

'Wait,' Tom shouted, but the bird flew further away, as far back as the dark canopy of the forest trees, and disappeared. Tom sighed to himself.

'Come on, our Tom, mother says you're to come in now and get yourself ready. Who were you talking to, anyway?'

Tom looked beyond the trees which stretched into the distance behind the little house. 'No one,' he said under his breath.

If that bird had really been his old friend Jollity the crow come to rescue him, it was too late now. The crow had flown off without even replying, which was odd. Then Tom heard the fatal clip-clop of the wedding carriage horses as they approached. He sighed again and made his way back inside the house with his shoulders slumped, bracing himself to 'get ready.'

Chapter 3

A JOURNEY TO THE LAND OF STORIES

'There,' said Tom's mother, 'now let's have a good look at you.' She stood back from yet another attempt to brush out his silly wild curls, and she looked Tom up and down. 'My, you look handsome today and no mistake, young Tom. I should like a nice portrait of you in that lovely outfit.'

Tom, however, felt very uncomfortable. He wriggled and squirmed. The collar was making his neck feel itchy. The special white satin knee breeches felt all slimy next to his skin, and the white silk knee socks made him look, well . . . ridiculous. His mother had forbidden him to touch any of his real proper adventuring things for fear of dirtying the white velvet suit. Tom stood as still as he could with his arms held unnaturally at his side. He knew very well what was going to happen when he stepped outside to where his brothers were all lined up and waiting. His mother suddenly produced something from a drawer in the dresser. It was a little gold coin mounted on a pin. She attached it to the lapel of the jacket.

'There,' she said. 'Your father found this little coin once in a very faraway place; it's real sprite gold. I thought it would be nice for you to wear something that once belonged to your poor father today, Tom.' And she sniffed and held back a tear.

'Thanks, Mum,' he said, 'but can I at least take my sword with me and my bow and arrows, and my adventurer's kit as well?'

'Now why on earth would you need all of that messy old stuff at a nice wedding, Tom Trueheart?' His mother shook her head.

'Please.'

'There really is no need for it at all, Tom.'

'I could just bring it all with me tied up on my packstaff,' he said. 'No one will know, it won't be in the way, and I might want to play, or get some proper bow or sword practice in later. After all, long speeches and wedding parties aren't that much fun for boys of twelve, are they now. *Please*.'

'Well, I suppose that's true enough,' she said. 'All right then, very well, if you must.' She shook her head. 'But be quick with you, they're all waiting outside, and for goodness' sake try and stay clean. Oh, and remind me, by the way, Tom, when there's a bit more time, to tell you something about your birthday sword.'

'Really,' said Tom, 'what about it?'

'I said, when there's more time, and that's not now.'

'Oh, all right then,' Tom said, and dashed up the stairs two at a time.

He put his leather tunic, his belt and scabbard, his three-and-a-half-league boots, a short bow and some arrows, a good roll of strong twine (always useful), his stout breeches, his cloak, his water bottle, and his wonderful, bright-bladed, sharp birthday sword, all into a length of Trueheart cloth. He wondered for a moment what his mother might have meant about the sword. Never mind, plenty of time later for that; he would soon find out. He bundled everything up and tied it tightly to the top of his packstaff. He looked one last time from his window out into the forest. He could see some birds wheeling far away above the tree-line in the distance, but there was still no sign of his friend Jollity the crow. He sighed and dashed down the stairs again.

He was already blushing bright red when his mother flung open the front door. Five of his six brothers, Jacquot, Jake, Jackie, Jackson, and Jacques, were all lined up in their best green tunics and fresh white shirts. Jack was wearing his traditional archer's jerkin. Jacques's face at first just turned red, and then he suddenly erupted with a huge shout of suppressed laughter. That set them all off. They roared and roared with mirth, and it seemed as if they would never stop. Jack even went down on his knees with his head in his hands.

Their mother, though, soon put a stop to it.

She called out to them all in her fiercest voice, 'Have you all forgotten who saved every single one of you from a deep dungeon in a castle above the clouds? Have you so quickly forgotten who kept all of your sweethearts sweet? Have you forgotten who it was enabled you to finish all your own stories? Have you forgotten the only one of you who fought single-handed with that awful Ormestone person in that dangerous flying contraption and won? Well, in case you have all forgotten, and so soon, it was this fine young man here, your youngest brother Tom, and a bolder, cleverer, braver boy never existed, so I will thank you not to laugh so cruelly at him just because I made him dress so nicely as a pageboy for your weddings.'

'Sorry, Tom; sorry, mother,' said Jack. 'It's just that we've never seen him so clean and tidy before, it was a bit of a shock that's all,' and he began laughing again.

'I said that's enough, Jack. Now come on into the carriage with you or we'll be late for the wedding.'

Tom climbed reluctantly into the carriage. He looked up at the weathervane and the roof one last time, but there was no sign at all now of his friend Jollity the crow. It looked as if his rescue would never happen, that his fate was sealed, that he would have to go through with the wedding, and be a pageboy after all.

The carriage set off, with everyone in high spirits, apart, of course, from Tom, but he couldn't let his embarrassment and misery show too much. He made a brave stab at smiling as they drove along under the canopy of the summer trees. After a while of rattling along in the carriage he chanced to look up, and his heart leapt, for he saw a crow flying behind the carriage. He watched it and it definitely seemed to be keeping up. As they turned through the trees along the twisty roads, the bird stayed perfectly in line with them. Tom's hopes of rescue began to rise again. He had tucked his packstaff ready at his feet just in case. He looked up at the crow again, but now he saw that there were two crows, and then they were joined by a third, all following the wedding carriage. While he watched, more of the dark birds appeared from among the trees and soon there were so many he could no longer tell if Jollity was among them or not, nor could he even count them. He pointed them out to Jack.

Jack looked at the birds. 'They're just a load of old crow-birds, Tom. Crows live in the trees all around here, what did you expect?'

'But they're following us,' said Tom.

'You're imagining things, Tom. It's those pretty breeches you're wearing, they're too tight and they've gone and addled your mind.'

Everybody laughed, and even his mother ruffled his wild silly hair fondly, then suddenly realized what she had done, and did her best to smooth it all back down again.

But Tom didn't feel the least bit addled. He watched the birds grow in numbers, until there was a whole dark flock of crows following their carriage. At the back of Tom's mind he knew that his old hermit teacher had once used a word to describe such a big flock of crows, and as he watched more and more of the birds wheeling in unison after the carriage he tried hard to remember it. He was still trying to remember the word when the carriage and horses drove triumphantly through the raised barrier into the warm and sunlit Land of Stories.

Chapter 4

The Story Bureau buildings were all covered with bouquets of white flowers. Garlands and wreaths and tributes of roses were scattered all over and among the trees as well, it was a perfect day for such a big wedding.

Tom's mother smiled to herself, she was glad that the Master had persuaded her to wait until the summer for the weddings, just look at all those roses. The scribes and devisers, the artists and puzzlers, the magicians and conjurers, and all the story effects people were lining the path up to the ceremonial Great Hall where the weddings would take place. All were in their finest formal robes. It was a vision of colour and light.

The Master himself stepped forward to greet the Truehearts. 'Welcome, one and all, on this happy day,' he called out, as they stepped down from the carriage.

Then, almost at once, another larger and more beautiful golden carriage drew up. It had last been used in the Cinderella story. It was pulled by six fine white horses. One by one the princess brides stepped down from the golden coach. First Snow White, then Cinderella, then Rapunzel, then Princess Zinnia (from the Frog Prince story), and finally the Sleeping Beauty, who yawned a little as she at last stepped down from the coach. The crowd cheered as each girl, dressed in a wonderful white dress of dotted sprite-silk muslin, took the arm of her brave Trueheart husband-to-be.

Tom put his packstaff down against the outer wall and set off behind the Master and everybody else as they all processed into the Great Hall. As Tom walked, a great dark cloud crossed the sun. The trees and the flowers all seemed for an instant to fade and darken. The colour and light went out of everything. Tom, who was the last to go in through the door of the hall, looked up and saw that the shadow was caused by the huge flock of crows as they passed across the sky. The flock had grown even larger now so that they looked just like a single black cloud, a cloud that blotted out the sun as they passed. He still couldn't remember what that word was for such a big flock. But, Tom thought excitedly, those birds were almost certainly some sort of omen, and not a good one.

After the Truehearts and their brides had gone into the Great Hall for the wedding ceremony, the enormous flock of crows settled in one great movement, and like a dark wave they fell across the roof of the hall. The roof was turned at once into a sea of shining black feathers. The birds settled themselves and waited for another arrival, just as they had been bidden.

Inside the Great Story-Hall every inch of free space was filled with the Master's finest roses. They were everywhere: hung in garlands across the big fireplace and even strewn and draped all over the great Storyteller's chair. Everyone settled happily in their seats. The Trueheart bridegrooms had taken their places in a proud line, along with their mother, in front of the platform.

Tom waited at the back of the hall with the princess brides. Each of them in turn had said how sweet Tom looked in his pageboy clothes, and one or two of them had even kissed him on the cheek and called him their 'little brother-to-be', which cheered him just a bit. It was his job now to escort the girls to the front of the hall for the actual wedding ceremony. Each of the five brides had a train on her dress which was made of the same sprite-silk muslin as the dresses but even lighter so that the trains floated like mist. All the brides' trains were linked together through a ring of fresh white roses and Tom held the ends of all the trains in his hands as if he were holding a cloud.

The Story Bureau orchestra struck up the special wedding march. The Master stood and raised his arms, and everyone else stood and Tom and the princess brides began to move forward down the aisle between the rows of chairs. Tom blushed bright red as he walked forward behind them. He felt his face must be as bright as a storm lantern, and that everyone in the hall was looking just at him. But of course they weren't, they were all looking at the beautiful brides in their beautiful wedding dresses. Tom could see Jack standing tall, a silly grin on his face and his arm around their proud mother, while she herself was busy dabbing at her eyes with a big Trueheart handkerchief. The brides lined up next to their husbands-to-be. The Master opened the big black book on the lectern. Tom's mother looked over at him and gave him a little wave.

'Welcome, friends and colleagues, to the Great Hall of the Story Bureau on this very, very happy occasion. We are gathered here to witness the coming together of these fine lovely young women and these fine brave young men, in their own proper happy endings.' He paused and beamed, looked around at the gathering and then added, 'A happy marriage.'

Everyone cheered. After the sound of the cheers died down there was a more mysterious and disturbing sound from outside: from high on the roof of the hall came the cawing of a thousand crows. People turned their puzzled heads and looked about them as the cawing noise died down.

'Before we begin the ceremony,' said the Master, 'I must, of course, ask a traditional, time-honoured, and very serious question. If anybody here among us knows any reason why I should *not* join these princesses to these brave young adventurers in marriage, then they should speak now, or for ever hold their peace.'

There was a moment of complete silence. Then the sound of the crows rose in volume again. There were wild jeering calls of 'caw, caw' as if the birds themselves were answering the famous question, and then the door of the hall crashed open with a thunderous bang, and a familiar chilling voice called out very loudly, 'I do . . . I know a *very* good reason,' and the Story Hall felt suddenly as cold as ice.

Tom noticed with horror that the rose tributes, the garlands and bouquets scattered all around the Story Hall, lost their petals in that same instant, and they showered down onto the floor like so much snow. Everyone turned to look at the open doorway. A dark fog of oily black smoke swirled in, fast, and someone screamed. Tom could see rows of bright yellow eyes through the smoke. He heard a low growling. Tom saw that it was wolves, the yellow eyes of wolves, a whole pack of wolves by the look of it. And standing among the wolves was a tall figure, looking like a black-clothed scarecrow with long white hair. It was none other than Ormestone, and standing beside him was a darkly dressed sprite, holding a gnarled little stick.

As the smoke rolled through the Story Hall, so the pack of wolves fanned out and circled the wedding gathering, growling and showing their teeth.

Ormestone spoke again. 'I know a very good reason indeed why these so-called couples should not be joined. It is not the ending that I have planned for them.' It was now so dark in the hall, and so thick with smothering smoke, that people were coughing and falling over in panic among all the growls and screams.

The Master called out above the fear and confusion. 'What is the meaning of this, Ormestone? You are banished, and most certainly not welcome here today, neither you nor any of your familiars. I ask you now, at once, to leave and never return, or suffer the consequences.'

'Why,' Ormestone replied, 'the only consequences to be suffered here are for you, Master, and your sunlit little land of so-called daring adventures, your safe cosy little world of fine resolutions and happy endings. For all of you here and your precious walled garden stuffed full of lovable talking animals, and swooning lovelorn princesses, and love-smitten swains, your flowery weddings and your Happily Ever After Island and your so-called Truehearted adventurers, I have important news. All of that will soon be over. Soon I shall return to this place with a huge dark army, an invasion force of horrifying ferocity. I will institute a whole new era, and you have all been warned. It will be the era of,' and here he raised his voice, 'darkness and winter and horror, and very, very, *un*happy endings. One by one other lands have fallen under our sway; why, only recently the peaceful green vale of the woodcutters was subsumed into our powerful darkness.'

He strode further into the hall, the smoke swirling about him, his wolves glaring and snarling at the gathering.

'For now, this one unhappy ending will act as an example. It heralds just the start of my larger plans; there will be many, many more such endings,' Ormestone continued. 'They will be endings which reflect the true realities of life, as it is lived. You are all about to see the first such ending in full operation.'

Tom's unarmed brothers had formed a hopeful and protective line, attempting to guard the princesses and Mrs Trueheart. Tom thought suddenly about his sword, and the bow and arrows and all his things wrapped up tightly and hidden in the Trueheart cloth on his packstaff. They were sadly and uselessly outside, propped up against the outer wall.

He began to edge towards the side of the building under cover of the choking smoke. There was a side door of heavy oak. If Tom could only reach his things he might at least be able to get his sword to Jack or one of his other brothers who would certainly know how to use it to best advantage. The hall may have been filled with smoke and shouting and growling and confusion, but alas Tom stood out all too clearly in his white clothes. He was only halfway to the door when he saw that a wolf had singled him out, and stood barring the way, its eyes glowing gold, its teeth glowing white, its tongue glowing red through the smoke.

Ormestone and his entourage had reached the raised dais. The wolves, so many wolves, surrounded the brothers and their princesses. Ormestone clapped his hands and the lead wolf nudged Jack forward, growling as it did so. The other wolves moved against the other brothers and their brides-to-be in the same way, so that a procession was soon formed of wolves and princesses and Truehearts. They were led past the astonished and terrified gathering back out into the sunshine. Another line of wolves, including the one barring Tom's way, moved all the scribes and the rest of the congregation, and Tom himself too, outside together in a big scared huddle.

A black airship floated on a tether outside the Bureau buildings. It had a huge skull and crossbones painted in glowing white along the side of its long balloon. A black gondola cabin was suspended from wires below the balloon. The gondola rested on the grass, which looked suddenly parched and colourless. The dry grass was covered over, as if by snow, with all the dead fallen white rose petals.

The group stumbled out together, Tom, the head sprite old Mr Cicero Brownfield, and the Master at the rear. They watched helplessly as the brides tripped on their tangled trains and dresses. The brothers cursed Ormestone out loud, but could do nothing, they were only too aware of the circling, savage wolves.

The Master whispered to Tom. 'I feared something like this might happen today, but this is much worse then I ever imagined,' he said. 'Cicero did try and prepare young Jollity, just in case; I have no idea if he succeeded.' He quickly pulled the Story Bureau ceremonial adventurers' sword out from his belt and handed it to Tom. 'Try and get this sword to one of your brothers,' he said. 'It was one of three special swords forged by your own father, you know,' he added.

Tom grabbed the sword. It was light and sat perfectly balanced in his hand. He felt a little flicker of energy travel up his arm as he held it. A sword forged by his own father, he thought; what else was there to find out about him?

The Master pushed him forward. 'Hurry, Tom, come on now, this may be our only chance.'

Tom took the sword, and made his way carefully through to the front of the terrified group. A spark seemed suddenly to fly off from the tip of the sword or was it just the sun dazzle on the blade? Tom was close now to the airship, which strained on its tether as if it couldn't wait to rise up into the air, taking with it the beautiful princesses and his poor adventuring brothers who stood surrounded by a pack of growling wolves. His nearest chance was the princesses.

It was Rapunzel who noticed Tom first. He held the sword up in the air, she called out to him and put her hand in the air, and he threw the sword over to her. It seemed to spark again, and then it flew straight through the summer air, end over end, in a graceful arc: Tom had been practising his throwing. Rapunzel reached up and caught it by the handle. Then she slashed through the train on her own dress, and rushed towards the ring of wolves surrounding her and her fellow brides. Sunlight flashed on the blade as she raised the sword high above her head and aimed a slicing blow at the nearest wolf. There was a strange sound when it struck, a kind of soft explosion, and a dense cloud of dark sparkles, and where the wolf once stood there was now a tiny sprite, his spell broken. The other wolves stepped back, their heads lowered, growling, with their teeth bared. One wolf sent up a howl of fear: suddenly it was their turn to be afraid.

Ormestone, his long cloak billowing around him, turned his head to confront the sword-wielding Rapunzel. He quickly shouted something to the little sprite next to him, who immediately pointed his stick straight out at her. Before she could dispatch any more of the sprite wolves, iron shackles appeared as if from nowhere, and snapped tightly across her arms. She dropped the sword in shock, and a trembling, growling wolf picked it up in its mouth. The little sprite, with a smile across his face, pointed his stick at each of the princesses and then at the Trueheart brothers, one after the other. Iron chains and shackles snapped across all their arms, linking them one to the other but keeping them very much apart.

Tom took his chance and ran back through the crowd to where he had left his packstaff. He tore off his pageboy velvet suit and pulled on instead his comfortable rough adventurer's things. He dropped the hated white velvet suit in a heap on the grass. He looked down at it and thought, good riddance at last, when the sun caught on the little sprite gold coin that his father had found. He bent down and picked the coin from the jacket: he wanted something of his father's with him and he tucked the coin into his packstaff too. Then he strapped on his own sword, hung his quiver and bow across his shoulder, and wriggled back through the throng to the front of the crowd. He hid behind a row of scribes; so far Ormestone had not noticed him.

'Nice try, my dearest, my beloved,' Jacquot called out to Rapunzel. He raised his shackled arms and tried to blow a fond kiss to her.

The wolf dropped the Master's ceremonial sword on the grass at Ormestone's feet. Ormestone picked it up and held it high over his head. It no longer flashed and sparked. 'Well now, I shall have a wonderful souvenir of this sadly failed wedding. Much more fun than a slice of tired old wedding cake. This is the ceremonial silver sword of the Story Bureau Master, forged, if I remember rightly, like another mystical and powerful sword which I also own, by big Jack Trueheart himself. I am sure I will find many, many, unhappy uses for this sword. How does the rhyme go; surely you must remember, Master? Down came a chopper and chopped off their heads, eh, what do you think, one by one, ha-ha. Well, I will save myself that treat for later.' He pointed at the dark door of the airship cabin with the sword. The wolves quickly herded the prisoners up into the darkness. Ormestone looked around at the assembled gathering, a big grin on his skull-like face.

'A new era has already begun. Indeed, it started some while ago. Soon, my Army of Darkness will arrive to lay waste this whole ridiculous place and subjugate all of you. I am afraid that my dear pets here,' and at this the wolves all howled as one, 'and I, must take our leave of you now. These charming young lovers have much to do for me, and much to learn before their final and very, very, unhappy endings. Farewell to you all. Come.'

A last rearguard of wolves formed a ring around the steps up to the gondola, while the remaining wolves scampered forward and slipped one by one into the cabin. Ormestone raised the sword again. He stood tall, framed in the doorway of the gondola, and it seemed he was about to loose the anchor rope, when Tom ran forward, right out into the clear space, heedless of the growling wolves. Tom had seen a chance. An arrow, if he could fire one of his arrows through the skin of the balloon he might deflate the whole thing and bring it down. It was risky, but worth a try. If he could keep them all down on the ground, there was at least the chance of a rescue attempt. He picked the bow from his shoulder, loaded an arrow, looked up at the huge black bulk of the airship and took aim. Ormestone saw him at once.

'Oh, wait now, if it isn't our old friend young Tom Trueheart. How could I have left you out of all this? Before you fire that arrow, my boy, just think for a moment. You have never had a story of your very own, have you? Which is a great shame; I think it is time you had a story all about you. I started a story here at the Bureau once, so far unused, which will suit you very well, I think. Why should your brothers have all the fun and adventure to themselves?'

Tom paid no attention to Ormestone, he just fired his arrow straight and true, directly at the hovering airship. One of the crows immediately flew down, and caught the arrow in its beak.

Ormestone laughed. 'Missed,' he called out. 'That was rather rude of you. No matter, it is time, I think, for your real story to begin now.' Tom heard his cackling, self-satisfied laughter. Then Ormestone swiftly loosed the anchor rope and the airship lifted off the ground.

The little sprite poked his head out from behind Ormestone's cloak and pointed his little stick wand at Tom. Before Tom could load another arrow from his quiver, he felt a sudden shock wave which rippled all

over him. Tom suddenly remembered something, at that exact same moment, before he slipped into the deep darkness of unconsciousness. He remembered the name for such a large flock of crows: of course, they were called a *murder* of crows.

There was a sudden horrible noise from above. The crows cawed and shrieked at one another, and beat their wings. Then they all lifted as one in a great wave from the roof of the Bureau and dived down and surrounded the slumped figure of Tom with a quivering black-feathered cloud. Tom's outline became blurred; he disappeared. The wolves that were left behind on the ground snarled and snapped at the crowd, and as the airship sailed away up into the sky the rearguard wolves ran away too, as fast as they could, back towards the far darkness of the forest. The murder of crows flew up at once in a great black cloud, once again darkening the clear summer sky.

The Master hurried over to where Tom had been standing. 'Tom,' he called, 'Tom, where are you?'

Tom's mother joined the Master. 'Tom,' she called, 'Tom, you can come out now, they've all gone.' But they could see no sign of Tom anywhere. It appeared that the birds had taken him, had somehow lifted him away with them.

Mrs Trueheart shook her head. 'All my boys, and all those fine, brave, lovely princesses too, and now my little Tom,' she said.

The Master nodded.

A single crow circled above them, a straggler it seemed from Ormestone's mass of guard birds, his murder of crows. The bird flew down and landed on the grass. Mrs Trueheart dashed forward and shooed at the bird. The bird stayed just where it was, and tilted its head on one side and looked at her with its beady eye.

'Mind where you're going,' the bird said to her, 'you might hurt Tom.'

She stopped and stared at the bird. 'Hurt Tom,' she cried, in alarm. 'Why, what on earth do you mean?

He's not here, he's gone, he was snatched away by all of you awful crow-birds.'

The crow waddled forward over the grass looking about him very carefully. 'I'm not one of them, Mrs Trueheart,' he said. 'Tom has suffered an enchantment,' the crow added. 'He must be around here somewhere, the poor boy.'

'Is that you, Jollity?' the Master said.

'None other,' said the crow. 'I couldn't show myself before, they would have recognized me at once, all those really evil sentinel crow-birds. They were the dark minions of Ormestone. Mostly criminal and rogue sprites under enchantments, I should think. Come on, we must find Tom. I'm sure he's still here, but make sure you look very carefully and mind where you put your feet.'

Chapter 5

Tom felt as if he had been hit by a bolt of lightning. There was a tingling all over, and then he was overcome with a sensation of spinning and giddiness. The sky and the cloud of black crows seemed to go round and round him until he felt suddenly sick. Then he fell to the ground in a dead faint. When he finally came to again he was in a strange place. Something wasn't right. He was surrounded by big clumps of earth and huge jagged rocks. There were very, very, tall green tree trunks. He stood up and shouted as loudly as he could. He ran forward through the surrounding jungle of trunks and giant plant stems. He jumped over a huge smooth white rock. It was like being in the dark eastern forest but somehow it was also very, very different. The tree stems above him swayed and rustled and roared and moved in waves together around him as he ran.

So, Tom thought, this is the Land of Dark Stories. He was sure that the crows had lifted him up in the air bodily and brought him to this legendary and terrifying place, the place where all the most frightening stories happen; the place where boys and girls leave home to learn fear. He was really scared now.

He dodged between the stems as fast as he could, in and around the huge green-coloured trunks. He needed to find out exactly where he was and what was happening, so he climbed one of the stems to look around. He clung on to the tip, and it was then that he froze on the tree top in horror. It was not only the Land of Dark Stories; it was also the Land of Giants. There seemed to be dozens of them scattered across the landscape, stamping about and shouting to each other above the trees.

A great shadow suddenly passed over him. He looked up and saw something above him that caused him to duck very fast. It was a giant white shoe, which passed just above his head, and only narrowly missed him. He slid down the smooth green trunk and lay hidden at the base. He watched the giant shoe crash down on the ground just in front of him, and the heel of the shoe only just missed crushing him. He sat up in shock; there was something very familiar about that shoe. He stood and turned to run as far away from the big shoe as possible, only to find himself looking straight into the black shining eyes and the open yellow beak of a big crow-bird. He fell backwards and covered his face with his arms.

'I've found him, here he is,' the crow called out.

Tom's mother leaned down and looked at the patch of grass near to where the crow-bird was standing. Tom pulled himself up from the ground, still in shock, and saw at once that the reason the shoe was familiar was that it belonged to his own mother; it was one of her wedding shoes.

She leaned down and looked at him from her great height. Sure enough she could see Tom. He was down among the grass stems and he looked suddenly to be about the size of a good man's thumb; he had suffered an enchantment, he had been shrunk.

'Oh my, Tom,' she called out. 'Is that really you?'

'It is him, I fear; he is under a terrible enchantment,' said the Master looking down from beside her at the tiny figure of Tom in the grass.

Tom's mother put her hand down towards him.

Tom, bewildered, stepped on to his mother's hand. She lifted him up level with her face.

'Oh, Tom,' she cried, 'my poor Tom, look what they have done to you,' and she let out a sob.

The Master's face appeared, as huge and pale as a moon, next to Tom's mother.

'Ah, Tom, there you are,' he said. 'A brave and

worthy try, my bold young adventurer.' His voice was so loud that Tom fell backwards on his mother's hand. 'You did your best but I fear you have suffered a malicious shrinking enchantment. I doubt we can do anything for you here. You will have to pursue that fiend and try to get the spell reversed in some way. Tom, you may be small, but I am guessing you are still brave and only too willing to help?'

Tom picked himself up and strode forward across the soft ridges on his mother's palm. He stood as straight and tall as he could. 'Of course, Master,' he called out. 'I will try to do anything that you need. But look at me, I am so very small, how could I even travel to the Land of Dark Stories, let alone do anything useful?'

'I can't imagine anything stopping you, young Tom,' came the voice of old Cicero Brownfield, and surely the crow that had so alarmed Tom was his old friend Jollity himself.

'Jollity, there you are at last,' Tom cried out, relieved to see his old friend and travelling companion.

The bird fluttered up into the air and landed on Cicero's shoulder, and said, 'Remember that snowy morning long ago last winter, when I told you you'd need courage, Tom? Well, I am afraid that goes more than double now.'

'I'll find double the courage,' Tom answered, but inside he was fearful and worried; how would he manage anything brave at all being this size?

The Master said, 'I am sorry, Tom, but we must plan your journey to the Land of Dark Stories. There will be two objectives: one to find and rescue your brothers and their brides; and the other, to stop the terrible invasion that Ormestone threatened, though how on earth you are to travel there and accomplish that I really don't know. Clearly it will take an age for you to walk anywhere being so small, and then there is the problem of the sea, it is a long voyage to that dark land. Perhaps we might slip you into the luggage or pocket of another traveller and get you somehow smuggled over the water that way.'

'No, no, Master,' said Cicero. 'There is a much simpler answer to the problem of Tom's travelling, to his journeying far away on this adventure, and it does not involve other travellers' pockets, or any kind of smuggling at all.'

'Really?' said the Master. 'Well, I for one cannot see it.'

'Neither can I, Master,' said the good-hearted Mrs Trueheart, shaking her head and sniffing back a tear.

'Show them, young Jollity,' Cicero said with a friendly wink.

The crow flew off Cicero's shoulder, circled a little turn in the air, and landed neatly on Mrs Trueheart's shoulder. The bird inclined its head down towards Tom and said, 'Come on then, Tom, hop on here.'

Tom stared at Jollity in disbelief. This bird was certainly full of surprises. What could it possibly mean, hop on here?

'What do you mean?'

'I mean climb on to my back, Tom, you will fit perfectly just in front of my wings here, and together we can travel as fast as the wind in the air, as fast as the air itself.'

'Oh my,' Tom's mother said, and raised her hand so that Tom was suddenly very close to Jollity. He leapt up as high as he could and landed square on the back of the crow. He slipped a little on the shiny black feathers, but he held on tight and managed to straddle the bird's neck, so that he soon found himself sitting comfortably across his friend's back.

'How does that feel, Tom?' Jollity asked him. 'Settled, comfortable?'

'Yes,' said Tom nervously.

'Hold on tight then; here we go for your first test flight.'

The crow took off from Mrs Trueheart's shoulder and lifted Tom into the summer air. Tom felt the rush of wind from the wings as he was lifted high above the Story Bureau. His stomach lurched and he was knocked backwards by the sudden speed as they rose up.

'Hold on tight, Tom,' the crow called back. 'You'd better get used to this.' And then the crow turned and swooped through the sky fast, tipping his wings down on one side.

Tom gripped the feathers hard and looked down at the ground far below him. He saw his mother, and the Master, and Cicero, looking up at them, and now it was their turn to look small instead of him. Tom felt he could get used to this. The crow soared up and down, round and round; Tom held on as best he could.

The faster the crow went, the more the wind blew Tom's wild hair back from his head, the more the tops of the trees rushed past them, and the more exciting it felt.

Tom could see the forest in the distance, with the dusty white road snaking among the trees. Further off he could see the edge of the forest and the shoreline and beyond that the sea, and, of course, beyond the sea somewhere far away was the Land of Dark Stories.

The crow finally spiralled down and then slowed in the air, and landed at last, very gently, on the low wall that ran round the Great Story-Hall. The Master, Cicero, and Mrs Trueheart came over to them. Tom sat on the back of the crow, smiling broadly now.

'You see, Master,' said Jollity, 'Tom and I can travel very fast together now. Nothing will stop us. We can be in the Land of Dark Stories just as soon as we are needed.'

'This will be a very dangerous mission, Tom,' said the Master. 'This will be your own story, not one belonging to your brothers or the princesses. It is clear that Ormestone has enlisted some dangerous allies; there are many hidden forces in that dark place. He means to have his terrible revenge and destroy us all. I am afraid he must be stopped in any way and as soon as possible.'

Cicero nodded his messy, leaf covered sprite head in agreement and Tom's mother dabbed her eyes with a corner of her Trueheart cloth hanky.

The Master said, 'We have faith in you, Tom, you know that. I see that all your weapons and your pack-staff have survived intact and seem to have shrunk along with you.'

'Yes, I have everything, my bow, my sword, my packstaff, they are all here, it's just that they are tiny now too,' said Tom, and added, 'like me.'

'Cheer up, Tom; you may be small, but I am sure your courage remains as large as ever,' said the Master. 'Go with Jollity, Tom. However badly you feel, this land needs your courage, and you are the only adven-turer we have left. Go then, just as soon as you are able. Do you know, your size may well be an advantage after all. You can get into places that would previously have been impossible for you. I think that our evil friend Ormestone may have just enchanted himself in the foot by casting that spell on you.'

'They surely cannot go yet,' said Mrs Trueheart. 'Tom needs to prepare himself; he should rest before such a journey. We have all of us had a terrible shock today.'

'That may be,' said the Master, 'by all means let them eat something. There is more than enough of the wedding breakfasts left for all of us, I am afraid. But then they must leave straight away afterwards if they are to have any chance at all of discovering where your sons and their brides have been taken.'

Mrs Trueheart nodded gloomily and prepared herself for a farewell.

Chapter 6

A Dangerous Adventure Begins

'Our adventure lies that way, through the forest, beyond the trees, over the Land of Stories, over the hills, and far away across the sea,' said the crow.

'I'm frightened though,' said Tom, 'frightened that I'll let everybody down.'

'You won't, Tom, don't worry. Now, have you got everything?'

'Yes, all set and all ready,' said Tom, checking his sword, his bow, his quiver of arrows, his shield, and finally his packstaff.

'Come on then, Tom,' said Jollity.

'Well, Tom, Jollity,' said Mrs Trueheart, 'time to say goodbye by the look of it.'

'Yes, I've got all my stuff here, Mum, look, my sword,

my shield, maps, everything. Now we're all set,' said Tom.

'Well, if you're sure,' she said.

'I'm sure,' said Tom, standing as tall as he could.

'Go on then, off with the pair of you.'

'Bye, Mum, goodbye, Cicero, goodbye, Master,' said Tom.

'Goodbye, Tom,' they chorused. 'And good luck,' the Master added.

'I'll look after Tom, have no fear, Mrs Trueheart,' said Jollity the crow.

'Oh, but I do have fear; I have six sons and five future daughters-in-law missing somewhere in the Land of Dark Stories, and soon my seventh son, my young Tom, will be there too. I have nothing but fear, my fine feathered friend, nothing but fear.' Mrs Trueheart shook her head and sniffed.

Old Cicero put a comforting arm around her shoulder.

'We'll be back, don't worry, and we'll bring them all back with us too, I promise,' said Tom.

'I hope you do, son, I really do.'

Tom held on to the back of Jollity the crow. He sank

his boots deep down into the crow's glossy black feathers and held tight to the crow's neck.

'Ready, Tom?'

'Ready,' said Tom, 'bye, all. Oh, and I'll look out for my dad too,' he said as he turned to face back to his mother and waved to her as the crow lifted off. They circled the Bureau garden with all the sad scattered rose petals, and Tom looked down and saw everyone looking up at them. He waved once more, and they waved back, and then the crow lifted higher into the blue sky, and he could no longer really see them.

Tom and the crow were soon flying over the dark forest. They flew high, swooping over the dark canopy of the trees. Then the crow flew up even higher, so that the shoreline beyond the enclosing wall of the Land of Stories was just visible, and beyond that the haze of bright blue that was the sea. Tom could feel the warm wind rushing through his hair, could see the ground passing fast below them. They flew on straight towards the coast and the wide open sea.

Tom watched the shadow of himself riding Jollity, as it floated and skimmed over the white clouds. They passed right through one of the clouds, and the strange soft light reminded him of that sudden feeling when the ground had finally vanished below him, on the climb up the beanstalk. Then, just like now, everything he had known before had disappeared below him and he had entered a strange new world for the first time. Only now he was the size of a thumb.

Although Tom was now shrunk down so small, Jollity was right, he was still a Trueheart. His own heart inside his little body felt as big as it ever was. Tom was excited now by the feeling of the wind in his hair, and by the sheer freedom of flying through the air so fast and of the prospect of a whole new story. A whole new adventure to explore. Although, at the back of Tom's mind, there was still that cold creeping feeling of fear, and dread, a dread that he would fail everybody. After all, how could someone the size of a thumb defeat anyone or anything bigger than themselves? He would just have to find a way, and whichever way it was it would have to be the Trueheart way. He was determined to stop the terrible Army of Darkness, to find and help rescue everybody, and of course to find out more about what had happened to his father and perhaps, if he was lucky, even rescue him as well.

Chapter 7

As Tom and the crow crossed over the Land of Stories, he could see all the important landmarks far below them. Almost in the centre stood the tall tower where he had seen Rapunzel for the first time, right next to the old tumbledown farm with its vegetable garden. The great beanstalk was, of course, long gone, but the huge hole made when the fierce giant fell through the earth was still visible as a deep giant-shaped scar in the garden.

They flew over the Western Gate and beyond that he could see the sea. On this fine afternoon the sea was as clear and as blue as crystal. The gentle breeze picked out white horses of foam along the tops of the waves, and it wasn't long before Tom and the crow found that they were flying over the Isle of Happy Ever After. This was where his brothers, and their princess brides, would have spent their honeymoons. It was a very beautiful green place surrounded by sheer white cliffs, a place of eternal summer. It would have been perfect for his brothers and their brides.

After the crow had circled the island he called out to Tom to hold on as he was going to fly very high. 'It is further than it looks on the map,' he said, 'to the Land of Dark Stories, and I fear conditions will worsen as we get nearer.'

The crow rose up almost vertically and Tom had to hold on tight to Jollity's feathers. They turned south and some way in the distance Tom could see dark clouds on the horizon.

The clouds grew bigger as they approached. After a while they loomed large around Tom and Jollity; they almost filled the sky with their dark grey shapes. Tom and the crow were buffeted by a sudden chill wind, and the clouds seemed to roll and boil inside themselves, like twists of dark smoke from some infernal machine. Every cloud they flew through was damp and cold. The fine summer morning had gone. It was colder, and greyer, and darker, the further on they flew.

Tom was shivering, and he had to bury himself deeper into the crow's feathers just to keep warm. They had left the midsummer idyll of the Land of Stories far behind, and were flying back down the seasons into what seemed to be a harsh winter. The sky had darkened around them until it felt like night time. Tom burrowed in tight to the warm feathers and drifted off to sleep. Jollity flew for a long while in semi darkness. When Tom woke later into total darkness he noticed that some of the surrounding clouds were tinged with intermittent flashes of red at their edges, as if there were a strong red light shining somewhere far ahead. The further they flew the stronger the red light seemed to get.

'Look out below, Tom, and you'll soon see the Lighthouse of Doom and the first jagged rocks of the Dark Lands,' said the crow.

It was then that a bright red beam of light suddenly swept the sky ahead of them. Tom kept looking ahead through the gloom and mist and sure enough finally below them he saw lines of jagged granite rocks that looked as if they had all been sharpened into points by a clumsy giant with a blunt knife. The rocks edged and defended the grim beach below like a set of dark red teeth. Looming tall on a rocky outcrop just off the shoreline among the dense rocks was a tall, dark lighthouse. The lamp was turning inside the tower, and the light that shone out of it was red. So strong and so deep a red was the colour that the sea looked almost black as it broke on the harsh rocks below, and the foam that splashed up with every harsh wave looked a sickly dark purplish pink.

'There it is below us, Tom,' said the crow. 'Welcome to the Land of Dark Stories. Hold on really tight, we're going in,' he added. The crow banked with his wings held out straight; Tom clutched hold of the feathers as they flew lower beyond the terrible sharp rocks towards the beach.

Chapter 8

A Grim Fate

Ormestone's dark airship had earlier flown on towards the red beams of that very same lighthouse. Fitful lights showed at the windows of the cabin gondola which hung below the long balloon. Inside the cabin, all slumped and chained together, sat an odd collection. There were brave adventurers, Tom's brothers, five of them in their Sunday-best wedding clothes, and one, Jack, in his rough archer's tunic. There was a huddle of beautiful girls, the princess brides-to-be, all dressed in their now sad wedding dresses. They were manacled together but in separated groups. The Trueheart brothers were down one side of the cabin and the girls were lined down the other.

The drone of the engines had sent one or two of

them to sleep, but most were awake and looking straight into the harsh yellow-gold eyes of the pack of guard wolves. Each group faced their own set of wolves, which were lined up, back to back, down the centre of the cabin. Some of the wolves stood alert and bushy tailed, others were slumped forward with their heads laid across their crossed paws; it had been a long flight. One pack of wolves looked over at the captive brothers, while the other pack looked at the shackled princesses. And each pack of wolves occasionally growled at their prisoners and flicked their white-tipped tails with impatience. The wolves had seen the one they called Rapunzel, had noticed her use of the ceremonial sword so finally and dramatically against one of their own, and they wouldn't easily forget it.

The Trueheart brothers had seen that brave attack too. Jacquot in particular had been more than impressed by the way that his future wife had handled that blade; it had been as fine a piece of swift decisive action and swordplay as he had ever seen. He had never suspected that a princess or a story maiden could ever handle a weapon, or indeed herself, like that.

There was no sign of Ormestone or of his

dark-clothed little sprite companion whose magic Ormestone seemed to be using so cruelly and effectively. They were somewhere up in the front part of the cabin navigating their way back to the dark centre of things. Occasionally one of the prisoners would try to speak, only to be threatened by a wolf. After a while the poor prisoners soon lapsed into a scared silence.

Jack was sitting very quietly and thinking hard, which was unusual for him. He had no sweetheart to worry about. He had no one at all to care about but himself, and he had no one to protect in particular. It did not matter much what happened to him after all. He felt himself to be disposable, so he had decided to do something, to take a risk which might help to free the others. With an absent expression on his face he had been working very slowly, and very quietly, with a little piece of sharp metal. He had found the sharp little fragment on the floor beneath him and had been sawing carefully through the manacle which joined him up to Jacquot and all the others. Jack was the last in the line of his chained brothers. If he could free himself from Jacquot, then he would be really free to try and do something when the opportunity came. Just where he was sitting the floor of the gondola had a curved structural brace which concealed his hands from the sharp-eyed wolf nearest to him. For the duration of the long slow flight he had worked back and forth on the metal of the manacle link. He could feel it weakening, could feel the metal warming and softening as he worked at it.

A sudden flash of red light filled the gondola. The wolves became excited. The ones that were slumped stood and shook themselves, as if they sensed the lights of home. They all howled, with their heads thrown back and their jaws wide. The red light came and went in vivid flashes as the lighthouse lamp turned somewhere in the dark ahead of them. Those brothers or princesses who had fallen asleep were now woken up with a start by the howling wolves. The gondola was suddenly full of confusion and Jack took advantage of it, working his jagged little weapon harder against the metal of the manacle at his wrist, but then the door opened at the front of the gondola and the little sprite assistant bustled in.

'All right, my beauties,' he called out, in his chilly voice. 'Calm yourselves, we are nearly home,' and then he licked his lips and laughed; it was a laugh which was as bad as Ormestone's chilling icy cackle.

Just then Jack felt the sprite iron of his manacle crack and finally give way, as Ormestone himself appeared from the cabin. Jack's hands were free; he was no longer joined to his five brothers. Jack hid his delight by scowling in the direction of Ormestone, and keeping his hands very still indeed. He whispered to Jacquot out of the side of his mouth.

'I'm free of my manacle, keep your arm close to mine when and if we should have to stand.'

Ormestone turned his head sharply towards Jack. He narrowed his eyes, and said, 'Something to share with us, Mr Trueheart?'

'No, nothing,' said Jack, putting on his best 'simple Jack' vacant expression.

Ormestone picked his way along the line of tangled wolves, patting their narrow grey heads as he walked. He came over and stood very near to Jack.

'Are you *sure* you have nothing to share, nothing clever to say to us?'

'Yes, I am sure,' said Jack.

'Sure what?' said Ormestone.

'Very sure indeed, your most illustrious, worshipful, magical, great highness,' Jack said proudly, defiantly.

The princesses giggled, and Jackie called out, 'You tell him, Jack.'

'I am the one to make any drolleries, any jokes, or little pleasantries here, and my little jokes and quips, my sharp barbs and jests, my tricks and spells, have a very nasty and very horrible habit at the moment of coming true, and you wouldn't want to be on the wrong end of one, I assure you,' he said coldly.

The red light flashed brightly through the gondola at that moment, and it lit up Ormestone's eyes suddenly so that he looked like quite the nastiest person Jack had ever seen. Jack felt a reassuring nudge from Jacquot next to him, which seemed to say, all is understood. Ormestone returned to the front gondola cabin and Jack waited for his chance. It would not be long in coming.

The airship suddenly banked sharply and began its descent towards the Land of Dark Stories. If he twisted his head a little Jack could just see the landscape out of the porthole by his head. The little sprite followed Ormestone into the front cabin and Jack was finally able to turn properly and look out of the port. He could see glimpses of the dark land below through the rolling grey clouds. The bleak landscape was lit by fitful flashes of the red light.

The cold voice of Ormestone called out from the front, 'Cabin doors to manual, crew, prepare for landing.'

The wolves howled in answer, and Jack saw the sharp pointed red granite rocks sticking up from a layer of thin, grey scrub. He saw forests of trees, with their bare skeleton branches all tangled up together, the details of their branches picked out in white frost. The landscape seemed to throw sharp hills and grey granite mountains up out of the ground wherever it could. There were dense forests, dull rocks, and wide flat plains. The monotonous flat plains were broken only by a series of tall poles with what looked to Jack like large cartwheels stuck up in the air on the end of them. It looked a miserable and frightening place.

As they descended to land among the dark shapes, Jack thought that they would soon discover just what kind of a story, and perhaps even worse, what kind of an ending Ormestone had planned for them all.

Chapter 9

THE LAND OF DARK STORIES

Tom and the crow flew on beyond the jagged rocks and the crashing sea. They found themselves flying over a bone-white beach. Tom could see a line of dark trees and spiky low shrubs and bushes. The trees were leafless, and their tangled bare branches stood out against the red light like row after row of frosted claws, or, Tom thought, like skeleton's fingers. Tom shivered as the crow swooped suddenly lower, aiming to fly under the beam of red light from the lighthouse. In fact the crow flew so low that they only just cleared, and sometimes had to dodge, the tangle of thorny shrubs. Tom felt them tug and scrape at his clothes. The huge sharp spikes of the vicious thorns felt to Tom as if they had a mind of their own and were deliberately targeting him, and trying to pierce his clothes, or his skin. He felt sure that they were ganging up and tearing at him. It was as if they were doing their best to keep him and the crow out of the Land of Dark Stories altogether.

There was a sudden 'squawk' from the crow and Tom looked up. Somewhere above them, a dark shadow flitted to and fro through the cold mist, lit up by the red light beam. Tom saw that whatever it was it threw a mysterious and frightening huge shadow-shape against the beam of red light. It was the hovering outline of a bat, with its sharp wings outstretched. Something black fell from its talons towards them in the darkness. Tom quickly raised his bow and loosed an arrow at it as it fell down towards them. He watched his arrow pierce whatever it was and the object floated and spun all the way down to the beach below them. The crow turned a circle in the air and then flew down to the beach to investigate. They landed near where the mysterious object had fallen.

Tom leapt off the crow's back. He scratched around on the dry sand, which was littered with fragments of spiky flint and sharp gravel, and which to Tom, in his new shrunken state, felt dangerously like big iron spikes and sharp shards of broken glass. A cold wind whipped across the beach, blowing the sharp grains of sand up and around in the air; Tom had to pull his neckerchief up over his nose and mouth for protection. His tiny fingers finally found the feather flights on his arrow which had pierced the middle of the object with its little shaft. It was a piece of thick paper. He called to the crow. The crow came hopping over and picked up the paper in his beak. It was an envelope, the same size as one of the Story Bureau mission envelopes. To Tom it was the size of a large carpet. This envelope, however, was different, it was made of jet black paper, and the writing on it was in a bright greenish-white ink, which seemed to glow in the darkness.

'FAIR WARNING'

it said across the top of the envelope in big capital letters, which almost seemed to shiver and move as Tom looked at them. Below this was another line of writing. Tom read it out loud as he walked along the length of the envelope: 'To whom it may concern,' Tom read. The crow dropped the envelope back on to the ground and stood beside Tom.

'That bat must have dropped it and then flown off,' said the crow.

Tom took out his birthday sword, and what little light there was rippled across the blade in a red flash. Tom used its sharp edge to slit open the envelope. His arm felt a faint surge of strength as he cut the black paper right along the edge with one long stroke, walking and pulling his sword hard after him. Tom could see a sheet of heavy folded black paper peeping out from inside. The crow helped Tom to tug the sheet of paper out of the envelope, and then they unfolded it slowly, the crow holding on to the edge of the paper with his claw. The same shivery-shaped luminous lettering shone on the surface of the sheet of black letter paper: 'Warning to trespassers,' Tom read aloud slowly. 'The sentinels now know you are here. Take warning, leave while you still can, if you stay you must accept the terrible fate that is very surely, and very swiftly, coming to you, signed King Ormestone, The Master, The Land of Dark Stories.'

'*King* Ormestone,' said Tom, almost choking through his neckerchief.

'Oh my goodness,' said the crow, 'he's calling himself a king now?'

Tom pulled down the neckerchief and stuck his tiny tongue out at the black paper laid out in front of them, and blew as loud a raspberry as he could. 'That's what I think of his warning,' Tom said.

'That's the spirit,' said Jollity the crow, while somewhere in the red mist, high above them, the large bat flew off fast and silently into the dark with an urgent message for its master.

Chapter 10

An Arrival

Darkness in the Land of Dark Stories

A few hours before, the airship had descended slowly on to a flat dark plain. The plain was dominated by one enormous dark building. Tall wooden poles and tall tree trunks, with all their branches lopped off, stood at intervals like a giant fence across the dismal space around it. The black airship was soon firmly anchored to one of the tall poles by a mysterious lurching figure. He had walked slowly and very deliberately out from the cavernous entrance to the huge building waving his red lantern light to guide the great airship in. The lurching figure, who was very tall and very broad and wore very thick-soled boots, pushed a wheeled ladder over to the gondola of the airship. He locked it in place and then waved his red lantern back and forth again.

The building he had emerged from was a strange mixture of styles. It was part cathedral and part fortified castle. It stood on a massive jagged granite outcrop surrounded by a deep abyss of darkness. It was made of dark granite stone, so dark in fact that at night it appeared to be almost black, and the only clue to its being there at all was the absence of stars in the night sky where it stood. The building consisted of a massively tall central tower which rose up almost to the height of the snow clouds. The tower ended in a crown of smaller pointed towers supported by flying buttresses. Dark stone steps and spiral staircases wrapped themselves around the outside of the circular tower. Outcrops and bridges, steps, staircases, and stone ladders of all kinds, loomed off the central tower.

Some of the arched bridges led to smaller towers themselves also wrapped in spiral stairs, and some just ended by jutting out blankly like traps for the unwary, stretching out into the dark air. It was as if the building itself had been designed as one big unhappy ending, for this was the Dark Castle. A tattered black flag flapped from its tallest, most pointed turret, from the very pinnacle of the crown of dark towers, and painted on the flag, in a glowing white-green colour, was a skull and crossbones.

The door of the airship gondola opened and Ormestone stepped down the ladder and stood looking proudly up at his ship, and at the far-off shadow of his terrible castle. His cloak flapped about him in the cold wind, and scattered flakes of snow drifted white across the shadow of the building and the dark sky.

'Bring them down,' he called.

Some of the wolves leapt down the steps and took up a position on either side of their master. Then the princesses appeared, one by one, and still chained in a line they stumbled down the steps shivering in their summer-weight, fine, white sprite-silk wedding gowns. They clanked their manacles as they gathered together on the ground under the ship. Some more wolves leapt down the steps followed by the brothers Trueheart.

Jack kept his arms close in against those of Jacquot and the others. Luckily there was very little light now. It was night in this strange and creepy place, so no one noticed the broken manacle at his wrist. Lastly the rogue sprite came skipping down the steps, waving his wand stick and chuckling.

It was Ormestone who finally spoke above the howling wind. 'Welcome,' he said, 'to my kingdom, a kingdom which is growing all the time under my inspired rule, complete with all new story beginnings, and all new unhappy endings for everyone. Here we all are, ready to make a new beginning or should I say, ending, in this kingdom devoted solely to dark stories. My assistants here will sadly have to keep the two groups of you apart.' At this the wolves moved forward and nudged and herded the Trueheart brothers and the princesses away from one another.

'My dear lovely young princesses here I shall leave for the moment in the trusted hands of my good friends the wolves, but of course my close personal assistant will visit them daily from his little house in the woods.' Here Ormestone gestured to the little sprite. 'He will be supervising you during your very long, and I am afraid almost certainly impossible, task to come. Have no fears, you will be well treated, there will be a chef and kitchen staff to keep you fed with delicacies, ha-ha,' and he laughed his cold laugh.

The sprite nodded his head up and down very fast, and then he rubbed his hands together with apparent glee. He looked along the line of beautiful princesses

then summoned the wolf guard and they began to herd them. The wolves pushed the princesses forward, and walked them away from the airship, and off down the road away from the huge castle. The sprite sat on a broomstick of hazel and birch twigs and flew up above them in a shower of sparks. He hovered a few feet in the air and then led the procession off into the darkness.

The girls marched away together tripping on their trains and tearing and ruining their fine wedding dresses as they walked. The brothers plucked up their courage and called out to them as they were taken away.

'We'll come for you soon,' Jacquot cried.

'If those creatures so much as touch you they'll answer to me,' Jackie shouted.

'Be brave, hold on, I'll save you,' Jacques said, 'we'll soon be with you.'

And then one of the remaining wolves leapt up, very tall on its hind legs, and placed its forepaws against Jacques's chest and pushed its snout tight against him. It looked up and growled fiercely, its teeth bared, its red tongue lolling and dripping. Jacques soon quietened down after that, and the brothers watched helplessly as their brides-to-be, the loves of their lives, the girls of their dreams, were marched off into the night by the pack of fierce wolves, while the little sprite rode on his broomstick.

It was to be a long walk in the wind and gusting snow towards an old palace which stood some way off. The old palace was surrounded by a high wall. Through a gate and beyond the wall was a stark formal garden full of spiky shrubs and dark evergreen trees cut into frightening shapes and one sad-looking scarecrow guard with a pumpkin head.

'They will soon be too busy to even remember who you are,' Ormestone said, and he turned to the lurching broad-shouldered man in the shadows. 'Come,' he said, 'let's get them off to the far dungeons, for early tomorrow you must start work way down below the very earth in my goblin gold mines.'

The brothers gasped. 'The goblin gold mines,' they chorused.

'Oh,' said Ormestone, 'I am so sorry, didn't I tell you, I have very important jobs for such a set of big, strong, brave, beefy adventurers as yourselves. And have no fear, you will not be bored.' And he laughed his horrible laugh again.

Then the lurching man stepped out of the deep shadow of the airship and into the full lantern light for the first time. He was even taller and wider than the Trueheart brothers. His face was covered over with sewing stitches; it looked as if he had been in some terrible accident involving lots of sharp flying glass, or indeed had perhaps even been stitched and sewn together from all sorts of bits of other people's faces. The brothers stepped back in horror at their first sight of him up close.

'Ah, I see you have noticed my strong helper,' said Ormestone. 'He will be your designated carer, the one who will be looking after you all on a day-to-day basis at the mine. He is a man of few words but he is, as you can see for yourselves, very, very, very strong, ha-ha-ha.'

The wolves nudged the Trueheart brothers forward, away from the steps, for now, and away from the huge dark castle. They could see on the dim horizon a pit-head wheel which stood eerily still. The wheel loomed darkly above the spiky dark trees of the forest, which were all rimed with sharp white frost.

Jack stumbled along after his brothers, keeping close to them, while Ormestone swished ahead of them all in his long black cloak. Jack could hear his cold chuckle as they walked. After a while the path fell steeply away on one side down into the dense dark forest itself. The ground looked marshy under the trees but hardened over with frost. There was only the one rearguard wolf trotting behind them, and Jack was the last in the line. He felt his only chance had come, it was now or never. Jack could hear the stamp, stamp, stamp, of the tall 'stitched-faced' man's big-soled boots on the frosted ground as he led the way with the red lantern, and the quieter rhythmic trudge, trudge, clank, clank, of his defeated and shackled brothers. Jack turned suddenly to face the wolf. It stopped too and glared at him in surprise; it bared its teeth and a low puzzled growl started in its throat.

'Now then,' said Jack quietly, 'look at this here,' and he leapt as high as he could in the air. Before the wolf could let out any sort of alarm cry, the skinny creature was knocked completely unconscious by the solid weight of Jack landing suddenly four square on the wolf's back, with his full force. The only sound the wolf could make was a very restrained and very quietly whispered, 'Oooof.'

'Well done,' Jack said quietly to himself, 'come on now, let's be away.'

Jack rolled silently off the path and then all the way down the steep slope over and over until he vanished among the cold mossy trees. The whole operation took only a split second. If Jacquot noticed anything of his brother's sudden disappearance he did not flinch or show it, and it was not until Ormestone casually glanced back down the line some many minutes later that Jack was finally missed. By which time Jack was running and dodging somewhere far off along one of the cold twisted paths in the vast forest.

Chapter 11

Tom and the crow soon left the beach and flew up and away from the lighthouse and headed inland. Below them stretched a wide plain scattered with occasional bare trees and mysterious tall poles which leant at angles to one another and often seemed to be topped by old cartwheels. There appeared to be something white stretched out across some of the wheels, but they were flying too high to see what they were.

They flew on through what remained of the night, and the landscape below them remained the same; a bleak grey plain broken by scattered lumps of sharp granite sticking up here and there, and clumps and copses, and sometimes wide forests of sinister dark trees. It was now as cold as midwinter. When the sun finally rose through the cold mist Tom could see no change at all in the landscape for as far as he could see, just another deep dark forest lay ahead on the horizon.

'Fly down a bit lower,' Tom said to the crow. He had noticed some more of the poles and cartwheels below and soon they were flying low over them. Tom wanted to see just what it was that was stretched out across the wheels.

He soon found out.

Once they were even lower, Tom could see only too clearly that they were human skeletons.

As they flew nearer Tom noticed a black crow sitting on one of the skulls. It lifted into the air and made a loud squawking noise as they approached. They flew lower still and Tom and Jollity finally landed on the rim of one of the cartwheels. Tom stepped off the crow's back and stood on the rusted sprite-iron ring which bound the rotten wood together. A skeleton lay across the spokes. It was stretched out with its back on the wheel hub and it was chained by the hands and feet. Scraps of ragged clothing were still attached to some of the bones, and they flapped and blew about in the cold wind; this was indeed a bleak sight. The crow walked forward and examined the skull which grinned back at him with its broken teeth and empty eye sockets.

'These are just staged frighteners, Tom,' said the crow. 'I don't think they are even real, well, not all of them anyway. I think they are just put here by Ormestone and his sprite henchmen to scare off any visitors, although I have heard that there is a whole army of skeletons here somewhere in this place.'

Tom turned away. He did not want to look too closely at the chained claw-bone hands, and the wisps of tattered prison cloth, marked with arrows.

'He wants everyone to think that this is the fate of all who are taken prisoner, that these are the remains of their bodies,' said the crow tapping at the skull. 'I thought so, it's nonsense, these bones are made of china. I expect they all are,' he added pecking at the claw fingers.

'Really?' said Tom. Encouraged, he climbed further along the wheel, and dared to look up close at the gigantic grinning skull. 'Why, so they are, all clean and shiny like a plate,' he said.

The crow tapped on the skull and it made a ringing clink just like one of Tom's mother's Sunday-best china plates at home.

'Just as I said, for show only,' said the crow.

Tom thought of that skeleton army; he somehow doubted that they were made of china.

All this time the crow that they had disturbed from the cartwheel had been circling over them letting out cawing noises. When Tom looked up he saw that it had been joined by several other crows, and that a whole cloud of crows was coming towards them from the far horizon where the forest began.

'I think we should leave, and fast,' said Tom.

He jumped on to Jollity's back, and gripped as tightly

as he could as the bird took off at a steep angle, pointing more or less straight upwards.

'We'd best make for the forest and lose them there,' Jollity called back to Tom, who could barely hear him for the rushing wind and the deafening sound of a thousand crows suddenly screaming at them from all around.

The cloud of crows darkened the grey sky, and the air was filled with their terrifying screams and the beating of their many wings. Jollity was knocked off-course and went into a fast dive towards the ground. It was all Tom could do to hold on. A stream of crows followed them down, twisting and turning in the air behind them. A menacing crow was soon flying beside them. Tom stared into its beady eye, and it suddenly pecked ferociously at Jollity with its beak. Tom drew his sword, and a tiny spark of light and a flicker of fire seemed to travel over the blade. It was gone in an instant and Tom was reminded in that moment about his sword, and something his mother had tried to tell him, but the sheer danger around them stopped him wondering any further. Holding tight to the twisting Jollity with one hand he slashed at the bird beside them. A flurry of cut black feathers filled the air, and then Jollity twisted upwards again. As they flew up Tom slashed wildly all around with his sword; feathers flew on either side of them, and screams and squawks filled the air.

The battle was on.

Tom found that by pressing his feet against Jollity's neck on either side, the bird would change direction, according to the pressure of whichever foot he favoured, and so he did his best to help steer Jollity through the mass of angry crows. They ducked and dived, charging through the cloud of birds, Tom flailing and slashing with his sword as best he could. As far as he could tell he simply damaged or wounded many of the birds as they passed through the centre of the cloud. Everything moved too fast for him to tell. There was no time to plan a blow, or behave like a true adventurer, with any kind of honour and chivalry. He just had to hack his way through and hope that they could keep going. The sword seemed to follow his hand and his wishes better than he could ever remember before, and he thought that he must, at last, be learning some swordsmanship. The line of twisted trees seemed a long way away still, and the wretched cloud of crows did not seem any smaller or less fierce.

Then the crows rose high above them as one. It was as if they had a single intelligence guiding them, telling them suddenly to flock together, and the sky darkened even more. The birds stayed high, following Tom and Jollity's progress towards the forest.

'They're up to something, Tom,' said Jollity.

'I know,' said Tom shivering. 'Fly as fast as you can.'

'I'm doing my best, but this is hard work, plus I think one of those birds injured me.'

It was then that Tom noticed some blood on poor Jollity's neck, and he could see a nasty gash under the feathers.

'Ouch, that looks nasty,' said Tom, putting his hand over the wound. 'Land as soon as we make the trees,' he added, 'and I'll look at it.'

They passed over a broad river; the water encircling what looked like a complete forest island below them.

It was then that the crows above them began their noise. It was as if an enormous alarm had gone off in the sky; a wailing shriek that rose and fell, up and down, up and down. It was just how Tom had always imagined that a banshee might sound, except that he had never heard one. His brother Jacquot had once, and had described the noise to Tom just to scare him before bedtime, and their mother had been forced to fetch Jacquot a swift ear-boxing for that.

Jollity flew ever faster towards the trees. It was all Tom could do to hold on. They flew especially low, almost skimming the river as they got nearer to the dark forest. Tom could clearly see the tangled roots of twisted trees, and the dank moss covering part of the tree trunks. Just before they reached the tree-line, in order to confuse the other crows, Jollity flew upwards again, and flew straight through the stream of crows hurtling down. Tom stood up excitedly on Jollity's back and swung his sword wildly.

Tom, however, was suddenly knocked off Jollity's back and spun through the air. He landed on the back of a strange crow which turned its malevolent head towards him, opened its beak, and screamed. Tom leapt up in the air in horror, for now he had lost sight of Jollity. He didn't know how, but he jumped from crow's back to crow's back, racing, leapfrogging through the mass of birds, defending himself all the while, slashing out with his sword.

Suddenly he was knocked from the air entirely by

a frosted tree branch, which seemed to grab at him and smack him like an icy hand. He tumbled towards the cold ground, his fall broken only by the jagged interruption of other sharp branches which he fell against one after the other. He finally hit the ground, and rolled into a little ball under a tree root. He lay there shivering and catching his breath.

The mass of birds carried on high over the trees, still wailing their terrible wails. Their arrival was certainly no longer a secret. The whole of the Land of Dark Stories would surely know that they were here by now, for the noise of all those crows had been enough to wake the dead. Tom lay as quietly and as still as he could. He had managed to hold on to his precious sword, and to his bundle, and had some scraps of food. How would he manage now, he thought, shrunken and pathetic thing that he was, and how would he ever find Jollity again?

The cloud of birds finally passed high overhead, and their sound faded away. Tom was left with the silence of the forest, which of course wasn't very silent at all. The bare branches creaked together, the wind moaned through the tops of the trees. Tom, being shrunken down so small, could hear the scurrying rattle and trace of every creature around him. Creatures that would have once been too small even to notice, were now to be feared: mice, rats, voles, shrews, badgers, foxes, all the wild things of any and every forest would find him a tasty little treat now. He could no longer fly above it all on Jollity's back, he was down on the ground, one small edible thing among all the other small edible things; why, even a blade of grass seemed as tall as a tree now to Tom. He would have to be extra brave, and extra cautious, and keep his wits about him.

He clambered wearily out of the dark root hollows, and all the trees moaned together above him. He started to climb a moss-covered rock, and even that was hard going as the cold moss was so slippery, and coated over with frost. Tom found it hard to grip with his little boots and he almost cried out in his frustration. He hated being small. The Master had said that there might be an advantage to being small at some point, but at that moment, in that place, Tom couldn't see what it was.

From the top of the stone he could see the huge forest stretching away on all sides, and a narrow path, that looked as wide as a broad highway to Tom, curved past the mossy stone, and stretched away on a zigzag route through the trees and far into the darkness. He decided that his best bet was to follow the path and see where that took him. At the very least he might find some shelter, and at best Jollity might find him again more easily if he stuck to the path.

So Tom slid down the stone, pulled himself up to his pathetic full height, braced himself, and set off wearily down the centre of the path. 'Come on,' he had to say out loud to himself fiercely, 'you can *do* this,' and so he marched away, putting his boots down on to the cold ground as loudly and firmly as a person of his size could manage. He kept his hand on the hilt of his birthday sword as he walked, and scanned the verges of the wide path for creatures, or for any sign of his friend Jollity the crow.

He walked further and further towards the trees until their twisted bare branches and tall trunks seemed to almost enclose him like a cage. It was so dark under the trees that it was almost as if night had fallen again. Tom had no lantern to light the path, and he could only just see the way ahead by the fitful light from the sky, which showed in patches through the branches. As his eyes and ears grew accustomed to the gloom, he noticed that there were constant scampering and twitching noises, and other worrying sounds from the darkness on either side beyond the path.

'Never forget where you are,' he reminded himself. 'And don't forget how to use your sword and your brain, and remember, normally those creatures out there would be more scared of you than you are of them.' But then he thought, This isn't normally.

He did his best to reassure himself, but deep inside his old fears of the dark had resurfaced, and doubly so now that he was so small and he found his walking pace slowing down. He felt that perhaps he might not be able to take another step. It was then, as he turned a bend in the path, that he saw a large sign. He looked up and read it out to himself: 'Welcome to Our Island,

The Vale of Woodcutters,' he read, and then he noticed a swatch of black parchment had been roughly pasted over the lower half of the sign. 'Warning: Now Incorporated into the Land of Dark Stories, So Keep Out,' was printed in the strange bright greenish-white letters ending with the image of a skull and crossbones.

So this was once a separate land, he thought, now taken over by darkness. It might mean finding sympathetic people at least. He trudged on past the signpost and at once noticed a distant friendly looking light. It was shining out from the window of a neat little wooden house, a house which looked very like the Trueheart house, and it stood just a little way off from the path. Tom clambered slowly up the steep bank, pushing his way through the tall tangle of sharp grass stems, and made his way slowly towards the light.

Chapter 12

Jollity flew upwards after Tom fell from his back. His neck hurt him where he had been slashed by the beak of one of the hostile crows. From his height he watched Tom skitter from one crow to another, leaping and dodging, bravely flashing his bright little sword. Jollity watched Tom get further and further away from him until he was finally lost in all the tumult of wings and feathers. Jollity flew lower by degrees and coasted over the forest. He peered between the trees for any sign of habitation. There were several woodcutter style cottages, set near and around the forest path. If Tom has survived that fall then he might go to one of those, Jollity thought, and he watched as the cloud of birds moved off as one across the forest. Then he flew down and settled on a high branch of a tree within view of the first cottage. He looked around at the roots of the trees. He was looking for something special. He soon found some, a certain kind of moss. He pecked at it, held it in his beak, and then went to tuck the moss among his feathers where he had been pecked at by the evil crow. This was an old wood-sprite cure for cuts and infections. He tucked the remainder of the moss under his wing and settled to rest, and wait to see if and when Tom should appear.

Chapter 13

A Welcome of Sorts
7.45 A.M.

Tom made slow and frustrating progress along the forest path towards the distant house. He could cover so little ground on foot being so small, and everything being so huge all around him. Pebbles and leaves were real obstacles to him now. He found himself clambering over the sharp edges of medium sized stones and having to walk around the bigger frosted leaves. This was certainly a very dense dark forest, the ground was scattered all over with crisp frosted leaves and pine needles. There were tall smelly mushrooms and toadstools, which were often bright-red capped and covered in white spots.

This is just the place for stray wolves and wild boar,

he thought as he walked but in truth he was more worried about the smaller creatures. Why, even a garden spider would be a fearsome thing to him now, and he looked nervously at the bright silken threads of cobweb that stretched between some of the ferns and plants. He kept his eyes peeled for any sign of Jollity the crow as well. He felt even more lost without him, and in this terrible place he realized that there was only one crow he could trust among millions.

After a good hour of steady hard tramping he finally walked up the path towards the cottage door. The cottage had a lean-to building at the side, which was a small stable, and there was a simple wagon and a friendly looking dappled horse poking its head over the half door. The iron knocker on the front door of the cottage was far too high for Tom to reach. He looked around at the porch, a trellis of rough branches all twisted together which went up on both sides of the front door. There was a shingled roof on top of the little porch, which had a pointed wooden finial in the shape of a bird which could well have been a crow. This was either a good omen or a bad omen; it was too soon to tell.

Tom was looking for a suitable foothold to start his climb up the trellised porch when the door suddenly opened, and a tall woman stepped on to the porch. She had an axe over her shoulder, with the blade end wrapped in sacking. She stood on the doorstep, and a smaller man stepped out beside her, holding a cloth bundle and a dark bottle.

'Here you are then, dear,' he said, and handed her the bundle and bottle. 'Your favourite today, a garlic sausage sandwich, with lots of mustard. And mind how you go working out there on your own in the forest, these are difficult times. Oh, how I wish we had a good strong son to help us now that we are older,' he said and sighed and shook his head.

'No mention of wishes, if you please, dear,' said the woman. 'Have you forgotten how things are now?'

'Of course not, dear,' said the man, 'but we did at least get a good strong faithful horse out of that first wish.'

'Sshh,' the woman said, putting her beefy finger to her lips, 'even the trees might have ears now.'

He lowered his voice. 'Well, I know that. She isn't much of a horse as horses go, and I know we must keep very quiet about that particular type of thing now, but she's been good enough to pull the cart anyway.'

'Yes,' said the woman, 'and that's enough about wishes for now I think, husband.'

'Bye-bye then, dear,' the man said, and kissed the woodcutter woman on the cheek.

'Bye-bye,' she said and made to move away from the step. Her husband looked down at the ground and let out a sudden scream.

'Stop,' he cried, 'stop, look at your feet, be careful.'

'What?' the woodcutter said, puzzled.

'You're still wearing your slippers, you silly old thing,' he said, and then he bustled back into the house and very soon came out again with a pair of proper big stout woodcutter's boots.

The woodcutter put down her bundle and bottle, and slipped her knobbly feet out of her slippers and into the boots, and then she shook her finger at him. 'And not too much of the old either,' she said and they both laughed.

'Ssh now, dear,' he said. 'Not too much of that laughing; not exactly encouraged by you know who.'

'Yes, dear, I know,' she replied quietly.

Then the woodcutter went to step again on to the path, and again her husband screamed out, 'Stop.' He pointed a trembling finger at the ground just beside her. 'You was going off without your sausage sandwich and your beer,' he said, and he handed her the bundle and the bottle.

'Thank you, dear,' she said, 'what would I do without you. Am I all set now, can I go off and get that horse and cart and start my wood chopping work?'

'Oh yes, dear,' he said, 'you're all set now. Bye-bye then.'

'Bye, dear,' she said and stepped forward in her big heavy clattering boots.

'Stop,' he yelled loudly for the third time.

'What is it *now*, dear?'

'Just look,' he said in a whisper, barely able to speak. 'Down there, stories be praised,' he said. 'Would you believe it, if another of our cursed wishes has not just been granted.'

The woodcutter looked down at the path and there stood a little boy not much bigger than her thumb.

'Good morning, missis,' Tom said. 'I wonder if you could help me?'

The woodcutter dropped her axe to the ground, handed her husband back the bundle and bottle and knelt down in front of Tom and said, 'I knew it, what did I say to you this morning, dear, all those birds, and all that terrible noise in the sky, it was an omen. Another of our rotten wishes has been granted,' she said.

'Sssh now, dear, that's just what I'm worried about,' said her husband.

She picked Tom up, and stood him on her hand while she looked at him.

'I am here on a mission,' said Tom staring close into the woman's face, while she stared back at him in wonder, shaking her head. 'I am here to find and rescue my big brothers and also their princess brides-to-be and also to prevent the invasion of the Land of Stories. I am Tom Trueheart of the adventuring Truehearts,' said Tom, and he bowed to her. The husband loomed up behind her, and they both looked down at Tom.

The woman said, 'He's trying to make little noises.'

Her husband said, 'My, my, this is not only one of our wishes come true, it is a sprite enchantment too. It's unnatural, we never asked for a *tiny* boy, just a *little* boy to call our own. There is a difference. No good can come of this, mark my words. We must take him straight away to the Dark Castle and hand him in, or it could be one those awful cartwheel punishments for both of us.'

Tom stepped forward across the woman's tough and calloused hand. 'My brothers were brought here in a big black airship by a certain Brother Ormestone and his pack of wolves and I need to find where they have been taken,' Tom continued. 'I am hoping you might have seen or know something.'

'Let's take him inside and have a good look at him. Let's give him some breakfast anyway at least,' said the woodcutter woman tenderly.

They had not heard a single word that Tom had said. He was carried in and set carefully down on a wide table. Tom stood among all the breakfast things. There were big wooden bowls and platters just like the kitchen table at home, except here there were just two of everything and now that he was small everything else, of course, was on such a giant scale. The couple sat at the table and looked down at him for a moment.

'Do you think he's real?' the man said. 'He could be just a clever toy or a puppet.'

'Ooh, he's a real boy, all right,' said the woman. 'You can't see any strings, can you?' She waved her big hand over Tom. 'And there's no clockwork key in his little back, is there. Couldn't you hear him just now, he was trying to speak, lots of little words, all of his own. Ooh, he's a clever little lad.'

The man put his hand on the table and reached out towards Tom, with his thumb raised, so that his thumb and Tom were soon standing up side by side. Tom was a little taller than the man's thumb, but he was not that much taller.

'He's our own proper little boy,' the woman said, 'just like we've always wanted. I shall name him Billy, Billy Thumb. Oh, if only we could keep him for our own boy.'

'My name is Tom,' Tom shouted, 'of the adventuring Truehearts.'

'Never mind all that about our own boy; it's time we were off with him to the castle,' said the man. 'We shall take him right away, you know I am right. Why, he might even be some sort of story start from somewhere else that got away, for all we know.'

Tom sat down in a sulk next to an egg cup, and he shook his head.

'Well, I think we should keep him,' said the woman. 'He's the granting of another of our wishes, after all. He might even grow in time, and let's face it, no one has ever noticed the sudden appearance of that horse of ours, and little Billy here looks so very nice natured, and he's very well equipped; look, he has his own little sword too and everything, and he bowed politely earlier.'

'You surely remember the proclamation they have just issued, now, don't you,' said the man fearfully. 'Anything like this, anything unusual, was to be reported, anything that smacked of granted wishes, or of possible happy endings, was to be handed in. We could be in very big trouble, my dear, if we don't do it and do it right away too.'

'My little Billy is my wish come true. I'll grant you he's forbidden, you're right there, but who would know we had him? We wouldn't be doing any harm if we kept him for ourselves, just like we did with our "horse"; and this time it's what we've really always wanted.'

Tom could stand no more of all this silly Billy talk. He had to find a way to be heard properly. He looked around the table. Hanging from the nearest chair was an old brass hunting horn on a strap. The mouthpiece was near the edge of the table and Tom simply crouched down and put his mouth to it, then he shouted through it as loudly as he could. His voice echoed through the brass horn, and erupted into the little kitchen very suddenly and very loudly.

'Listen to me, please,' he said.

The couple sat up and took notice at that.

'My word, he *can* speak, and real words too,' said the man in a quavering, 'worried more than ever', voice.

'Course he can,' said the woodcutter. 'Billy's a very clever little fellow, dear.'

'I'm not the answer to anyone's wishes,' said Tom as loudly as he could. 'I am named Tom, Tom Trueheart.'

'Told you he was called Tom, Tom Thumb, didn't I say, dear,' said the woman.

'You said he was called Billy,' said her husband.

'To repeat,' said Tom, 'I am one of the adventuring Truehearts, I am here to rescue my brothers and their princess brides from wherever it is they have been taken.'

'Well, as you can see, we have no brides and no brothers here,' said the man. 'We are but a humble woodcutter and her poor husband, trying to earn an honest living in dangerous times. We just want to carry on living our quiet life here in the forest, without bothering anyone else at all. We don't care for adventure, and we want no trouble here from the army.'

Tom interrupted him. 'Perhaps you would help me then,' he said. 'I am here to stop the Army of Darkness invading my own land just as yours has been.'

'A word, wife,' the man said, and he pulled the woodcutter up and away from the table.

They went off to the other side of the room, and began an urgently whispered conversation.

At first Tom could hear nothing of what they were saying, but then he put his head into the mouthpiece of the hunting horn, and soon found he could hear every word that they said.

'He's a danger to both of us,' the husband was saying. 'You know full well what was written on that proclamation. Any hint at all of a granted wish, any sniff of a dream come true, was to be reported at once to the castle. It's not our fault, we don't make the rules. You've seen what's on them cartwheels stuck up all over the place.'

'My friend the forester says they're not real,' said the woodcutter, 'they are just made of old china plates and bowls, he says.'

'He'd tell you anything that one, I know his game. Don't you listen to him, the law is the law, and we must hand this lad in.'

'Well, it's come to a pretty pass when all the things you've been wishing for over all these years finally seem to be being granted, one by one, only to have them taken away from you straight away,' said the woodcutter sadly, shaking her head.

The man shook his head too. 'You're too good-hearted, that's always been your trouble, dear.'

The woman looked at him with a sad expression on her face. 'Come on then,' she said, 'let's get on with it.'

So without further ado Tom was lifted off the table and taken outside. The dappled horse was fitted into the wagon shafts, and Tom was wrapped up tightly in a warm wool scarf.

'I hope you are warm enough; we haven't had even a hint of summer since *the King* arrived,' she whispered. 'Here, you can sit up beside me, my little Billy, sorry, my Tom Thumb, for a nice little while at least.'

The husband locked up the little house and went and settled himself on the back of the woodcutter's cart. Tom was settled beside the woodcutter, and they set off.

They trotted away from the warmth of the wood-cutter's cottage and out into the big cold forest. Tom looked around at the avenues of seemingly endless trees as the horse clopped along the mazy path under the dark grey sky. Here he was with the strange wood-cutter and her husband, who would soon hand him in. Tom would have to bide his time; he saw no chance of escape just yet.

As the cart trundled on its way through the forest it was followed, high in the air and at a safe distance, by a lone crow.

Chapter 14

The Old Palace
9 A.M. SHARP

The princesses were all lined up on a balcony, the minstrel's gallery of the old palace. In front of each of the princesses, there stood a lurid green wooden spinning wheel. The rest of the big room below them was filled from top to bottom with a huge mound of straw, which was the size of a haystack. It bulged upwards in a great pile and at its pointed top it nearly touched the ceiling above them. Ormestone paced up and down behind the young women accompanied by a pair of exceptionally fierce and growling wolves, each wolf with a white tip to its tail. Ormestone spoke coldly.

'While your lumpen and doltish "might have been", but never "will be", so-called "adventurer" husbands-to-be are hard at work in my deep goblin gold mines . . . '

At these words the girls all gasped. They each had a good idea of just exactly what a goblin mine might be like.

'Oh, I am so sorry if I have surprised you. Didn't you know? Yes, they are very, very, very busy, deep down, probably even under our very feet, somewhere in the heat and darkness, chipping and digging, hacking and tunnelling, just looking out for fine gold seams for me, and very obliging of them it is. I am sure they are all wondering exactly what you are up to too. Indeed, I expect you are yourselves wondering why you are here, and why I have arranged all this.' And here he swept his arm around the room, indicating the garish spinning wheels and the straw.

'They have been prepared especially for you.' He pulled an envelope out of his cloak. He tore it open and he took out a letter written on fine creamy foolscap parchment. It was a Story Bureau letter.

'Well now,' he said, 'as you know I recently paid a flying visit to the Story Bureau, back in your pretty Land of Stories. I found all sorts of interesting things there, and I am afraid I helped myself to them. I brought them back here with me. There were secret letters to adventurers, story notes, and amongst it all was this new story start which gave me this idea. The story was to be about a humble miller's daughter. I thought we might start this particular story today; rather a demotion I am afraid for all of you. Now what exactly does it say? Ah yes, it appears that her father has been bragging to the king that his daughter could spin straw into gold. Can this be true?'

The girls stayed silent, not one of them would give Ormestone the satisfaction of being rattled by, or appearing interested in, his silly performance.

'By your defiance, I may take that as a yes. I am so glad, for I am very much in need of sprite gold and lots of it, for my many plans. What could be more sprite-like, more charming, than the thought of all you enchanted princesses sitting in here all day and all night spinning, and spinning all of this base straw into the most delicate gold, as only you apparently can. You must not disappoint your king, must you? I think for the purposes of this story I can safely be thought of as the king. I shall expect to see a lovely pile of pure sprite gold all piled up here by tomorrow morning. Oh, and, Sleeping Beauty, you have a care now with that spindle, we wouldn't want to go through all that awful sleeping for a hundred years again, would we? Especially now that there is no one to wake you up with a kiss, for after all I have captured the princes and cancelled all the possible romantic happy endings. In short, to put it bluntly, I want a big pile of sprite gold, here at seven a.m. sharp tomorrow. Come, my hounds,' and he swept down the staircase with the wolves.

He paused at the bottom. 'Oh,' he said, 'and don't even think of running away. My personal guard hounds will be just outside these heavily padlocked doors, and my trusty sprite will be with you very soon, just as I promised. He will be here every day to see how you are getting on, supervise your meals and so on. He may be small but he is very powerful; I should be very careful how you behave with him. You know full well what his powers can do.'

With that Ormestone was gone, leaving just the one wolf slumped at the bottom of the stairs. They all heard the key turn in the lock, and then there was silence, apart from the low rumbling growls of the guard wolf.

'Oh, that awful man,' Rapunzel said.

'He's hideous,' said Princess Zinnia.

'Vulgar,' said Cinderella.

'So cold,' said Snow White.

'Makes me feel scared and sleepy at the same time,' said Sleeping Beauty, 'and whatever shall we do with all this? I can't spin straw into gold.'

'I can't spin anything,' said Zinnia.

The others all agreed that they couldn't spin anything either, and had not the first clue how to begin.

'Well,' said Sleeping Beauty, 'I remember that I once went high up in a haunted tower, it was at my home castle; I just wanted to learn how to spin. I was lured there on my sixteenth birthday by a bad fairy who meant me harm, but I didn't get very far in my spinning lessons because I pricked my finger on the spindle and fell asleep straight away. It was supposed to be for a hundred years; well, it would have been if a certain young—'

'Yes yes,' said Princess Zinnia, 'never mind all that, we all know the story by now. Clearly you are going to be no use to us, and don't set us off, for goodness' sake, with all the romantic stuff. The question is, what shall we do now?'

'Our duty is to escape, find our poor husbands-to-be, and rescue them, and fast,' said Rapunzel.

'Agreed,' they chorused.

It was then that the guard wolf growled a little louder from the stairs, as if just to remind them of the absolute impossibility of escape.

'Look at all that straw,' said Cinderella with a sigh. 'You forget that I am used to hard work. Why, I spent what seemed like for ever grubbing out sooty fireplaces and the like, and at least the straw looks clean.'

'We are meant to turn it into gold, not wash the floor with it,' said Zinnia.

'I'm not even bothering. After all, what is the worst that awful creep Ormestone can do to us?' asked Rapunzel.

'It's not what he might do to *us*,' said Zinnia, 'it's our poor, lovable, silly Trueheart men, the loves of our lives, and what he might do to them that we should be worrying about.'

The princesses were silent for a minute, while they considered that horrible thought. It was just then that they heard a clanking rattle at the lock on the door. The wolf sat up, growling and showing his teeth, and then the door opened, and when the wolf saw who was coming through the door, he stopped growling and sat down again. It was the shabby little sprite that had piloted the airship with Ormestone. He slipped up the stairs like smoke, like a bad smell.

'Good morning to you, all my ladies,' he said.

He found the princesses sitting in a line at their spinning wheels, looking as if they were busily at work, as if they knew what they were doing.

'Goodness me,' he said, 'what a lot of straw, and so many spinning wheels. What are you doing?'

'As if you don't know,' said Zinnia.

'My, my, you really shouldn't frown in that way, my princess. What if the wind changed? Those lines might stay across your forehead for ever like that and that would be a shame.' And he chuckled. Then he suddenly jumped over the edge of the balcony and landed light as a feather on top of the huge heap of straw.

'I can watch you all so nicely from here, so busy at your task. Remind me again what it is you must do?'

'We must spin all that straw into gold; no, into *sprite* gold, for the so-called king.'

'Sprite gold,' he said, 'really? The most delicate, the most beautiful, the most precious substance in the Land of Dark Stories, and you must spin it out from all this old straw?'

'Yes, just that,' said Cinderella.

'Well,' said the little sprite, 'very good luck to you all. Of course, if you were very, very, very, very, very, very, very, *very* nice to me, I could possibly help you with this task much more than you know.'

Part Two
Towards the Dark Castle

Chapter 15

Jack lay low for an hour or so. He hid in a hollow among some very thickly knotted tree roots. 'I wonder if he'll send those wolves out after me?' he said to himself, shivering in the early morning chill. 'They won't have noticed I've gone yet, with any luck. What I'll need though, just in case they do, is a good weapon, for defence. Now don't forget it, Jack.'

Jack trudged on through the night forest. After a while he stopped for a rest, and by and by he fell asleep. When at last the sun rose, Jack woke up and found that snow had fallen in the night and was piled up on him and around him in drifts and patches. Jack stood and shook the clumps of snow from his tunic. He waved his arms and stamped his feet.

'I swear it was midsummer when we were snatched away,' he muttered, shivering miserably. 'Well, I've got me some drinking water at least,' said Jack, scooping up a handful of snow in his hand.

Then Jack remembered his need for a good weapon. He poked about among the trees. 'I must choose just the right thing, you see,' said Jack under his breath. 'Ah, here we are, a nice piece of good dry oak.' Jack broke a straight branch off in his hand. It was about his height. He sat down on a nearby stump and pulled the little piece of sharp metal out of his tunic.

'Very useful, this scrap I found. I hacked through that sprite manacle with it and now it will help me to make a proper weapon. Now, I've got to make the centre of this thicker than the top and bottom, see?' Jack set to work scraping at the hard oak, shaping and refining. 'I'll just shave the ends here a little to give it a bit of flexibility,' he said quietly, concentrating hard on his task. He took the metal tool and cut vee-shaped notches in the curved ends of the length of wood. He flexed it. 'There,' he said, 'good and springy, now for the next bit.'

He put the piece of wood down against a tree stump. To warm himself up a bit, he strode around awhile looking through the patchy snow on the ground for straight sticks, all about half the length of the one he had just worked. 'Really straight ones, mind, sharp dead straight, no curves, no bends,' he said.

He collected a good bundle of hard straight sticks then spent a happy few minutes sharpening the ends of them. Then he sat and cut notches on the blunt ends of all the sharp sticks. Then he stripped some bark from a tree sapling and fashioned a holder for the sticks. Jack stood and walked around again. He looked at the sheltered patches free of snow near the tree roots and scooped up some of the many shiny black crow feathers that littered the ground.

'I don't like this forest,' he said quietly, 'it's too dark, and too cold, and there are some very odd noises all around the place. I swear I heard wolves howling somewhere nearby. Mind you,' he added, 'this is the Land of Dark Stories, after all. I should think that there are more wolves right here in this very forest than almost anywhere else on earth. Hang on now, I keep talking to myself; time to stop that.'

Jack had all the while been stripping and plaiting some more bark from yet another sapling, and had fashioned a good length of a very tough kind of string. He looped the string through the notches on the tall stick and fixed it tight so that the stick bent into a taut curve. He plucked the string just a little so that it twanged with a deep note. He attached some black crow feathers to one of the sharp notched sticks. He raised the tall curved stick with his left arm held straight out, and then he slipped a sharp stick against the tight string and pulled it back with his right hand. He fired the stick into one of the trees. It landed with a loud thunk and just quivered there.

'A good stout longbow and arrows,' said Jack, 'an adventurer's weapon of choice.'

He made a reasonable breakfast out of some gathered nuts and berries and a few crab apples and he washed it all down with a good draught of snow-melt. After breakfast he had decisions to make.

What do I do now? he thought looking around among the dense trees. First orientate myself, find the road, and establish a direction, then set off on a search and rescue mission. I am a Trueheart, of the adventuring Truehearts, after all. Now normally, of course, I would have a nicely written out Story Bureau letter which would set me off on my adventure. Today I have no letter, no story start, no instructions, no map, nothing, but I have been an adventurer long enough to know this. My brothers and their brides have been taken off by that awful Ormestone and his pack of wolves. Taken to some awful place somewhere here in the Land of Dark Stories where nothing but unhappy endings wait for them. It's up to me to do something about it. Come on then, Jack, brace up, off I go on a nice new rescue adventure. I shall travel eastwards, this way where the sun rose. I am sure to hit a road soon, and then a crossroads, and then I shall see what to do. I'll take it a piece at a time.

So Jack put his new bow across his shoulder, tucked his full quiver of arrows on to his belt, and set off through the patchy snow, with a heart full of adventure, and a belly half full of nuts and berries.

Chapter 16

The five remaining Trueheart brothers, all manacled together, were shivering and walking
awkwardly forward, wolves snapping at their heels, on
that very next dark cold morning. Ormestone's
henchman, the man with the face that looked as if it
had been sewn together from other faces, was herding
them all towards a mine shaft. They could see a waiting
lift cage and the dark broken wheel. Ormestone had
left an envelope for them in their dank dungeon near
the mine. It was exactly like a Story Bureau envelope,
except that the paper was black, and the writing was
white. It was a letter from the King of the Land of Dark
Stories. It said that they would be 'taken to a gold mine,

run by trolls and goblins, and once there they would work the most difficult remaining mineral seams until all were completely exhausted.' It was not clear from the letter whether it was the Trueheart brothers or the mineral seams themselves that were to be exhausted.

There was no sign in the early morning cold and frost of Ormestone himself. The stitched-faced man pushed the brothers into the tiny lift cage with grunts and shoves. Jacquot noticed that there seemed to be a metal bolt visible in his neck. The man never spoke, he just grunted and made moaning noises. He shut the gate, locked the padlock, and then handled the huge lift rope, hauling it over a pulley, so that the lift cage, full of Truehearts, began its descent into the gold mine.

The brothers watched him as he tirelessly hauled the rope through his huge hands while they were lowered into the darkness. Once he was out of sight they began to speak; and all at once.

'I hope our girls are all right,' said Jackson.

'He'll wish he'd never been born if he's harmed them,' said Jackie.

'I saw a troll and a goblin once,' said Jacques, 'they weren't pretty.'

Jacques was soon proved to be telling the truth. Once the cage reached the bottom of the shaft they could see tunnels stretching away on all sides lit with flaming torches and lanterns. They could see groups of smallish hunched creatures pushing mine carts. It was suddenly very hot. A grinning creature unlocked the cage door.

'This way, if it please you, his fine strong gentlemen,' the creature said, bowing a little as it opened the door. It stood at half the height of a Trueheart, and gave a little laugh as they filed and shuffled out into the cavernous gold mine. The laugh would have curdled a jug of Mrs Trueheart's finest fresh milk; it was a laugh fit to freeze the blood. This was a goblin, and that was a goblin laugh, and like all goblins it had wet looking, greenish skin.

'Welcome to the Trollgild mine. He will take you to the gold seams where you will work. He will give you the six shovels and the six picks and the six carts and the six lanterns, and he will send the trolls to guard the gold.'

'Who the blazes is "*he*"?' asked Jake defiantly. 'And why six shovels when there's only five of us here?'

'Why, *I* is he,' said the goblin, and looked down at a sheet of black paper in his hand. 'Says six here on this list from the king.'

'One of us escaped last night,' said Jake with a smile.

The goblin said, 'They'll soon find him,' and laughed again, only louder this time, so that some of the Trueheart brothers were forced to try and cover their ears, which was hard to do as they were all still manacled and chained together.

'This way,' said the goblin, and he slipped forward down a side tunnel like a damp toad.

A huge troll was crouched in the tunnel picking through some chunks of ore and rock which were piled up in a mine cart. He turned his head and watched the Truehearts as they approached. He was two and a half metres or so tall, and he had a long beard which draped down his chest, and long hair covering part of his face. His eyes were huge and were so pale they were almost white. This was a creature that had lived and worked in the dark underground for a very long time.

Jake thought that his own eyes would end up like that if he was left down here for long enough.

'Gold,' the troll said as they passed him. 'Gold good.'

'This troll watches you all; no stealing troll gold, the king's gold, Ormestone's gold,' said the goblin. 'Only hard work for you here. He gives you *five* shovels now, he gives you *five* picks now, he gives you *five* lanterns now, he tells you to work now, and then he goes away. But remember troll watching, make sure, troll like to eat people.'

The goblin laughed again, showing his tiny sharp jagged teeth, and their blood froze again. The goblin waved his hand vaguely and the manacles on their arms vanished. The troll looked over at them and licked his great lips. Then the goblin was gone. He had skittered away somehow in the hot stifling darkness, leaving just a line of picks and shovels and candle lanterns propped against the mine carts by the tunnel wall.

Jacquot rubbed his arms and said quietly, 'Look, we've got weapons now, and no manacles, so here's our chance. What's to stop us bashing a few heads in and getting out of here?'

'Me what to stop you,' said a deep gravelly voice from the darkness behind them, and another, even bigger troll shuffled out of the looming shadows and stood over them.

'Guard troll, guard gold, guard you too.'

'Forget that idea then,' said Jake.

After that they worked on for hours, and hours, and hours, hacking at the mineral seams with their picks, scraping out the glittering chunks of ore, and shovelling it all into the mine carts.

The goblin returned much later with a bucket of gruel and some hook-handled cans to drink it with.

'He gives you the five cups, he ladles out the five portions of Trollgild gruel, good for work, good for muscles,' said the goblin, and laughed his blood-freezing, milk-curdling laugh again.

The gruel tasted just a little the way you might imagine that a trail of slime left by a big fat yellow slug on a wet day in the garden might taste. Only at the same time, it was also chewy and gritty, like a mouthful of sand, as well. They had to force themselves to eat it.

It was going to be a very long day.

After what seemed a whole week had passed, a bell rang, and the troll took the brothers' shovels and picks and lanterns away from them. The goblin raised his hand, yawned lazily at the brothers, and the sprite-iron manacles snapped back across their arms, and then they were led back through the low tunnels to the deep chamber by the goblin.

'He puts you all back in the cage, he counts you, one, two, three, four, five, not six yet but soon. He locks the cage, he sends them all away until tomorrow. Five silly Truehearts locked in a cage, puts all the Bureau in such a rage,' and again he laughed his horrible laugh. Another bell sounded somewhere on the surface.

The exhausted Truehearts stood all crammed together and dirty in the hot cage as it was pulled jerkily up to the surface again.

'What a day,' said Jacquot.

'We've got to do something about this. We can't go doing this for ever, we'll be worn out and finished off in a week,' said Jake.

'Well, that was definitely the worst day, and the worst job ever, ever, ever,' said Jackson.

'What, worse than being a little frog, *riddip*,' said Jacques who managed a little snigger after he had said it.

'Oh, I see, you can't let that one lie, can you, any of you. All right, I admit it, I was once a frog. Get over it,' said Jackson crossly.

'Now now,' said Jackie, 'let's not quarrel, it'll only make it worse for ourselves.'

'You're right, sorry, Jackson,' said Jacques.

'Group hug,' said Jackson brightly.

The brothers huddled together, their arms wrapped around as many of each other as they could get hold of. They may have been exhausted, damp, and smelly, and full of the awful Trollgild gruel, but they were Truehearts, after all.

'With a true heart,' Jackson said quietly.

'With a true heart,' came the exhausted chorus of

tired but defiant brothers in reply, as the lift cage shuddered to a halt at the mine entrance.

'We'll get out of all this soon, mark my words. Never forget that our Jack has escaped, he is free, and he will be looking for us. He could be coming to rescue us even now, and who knows what young Tom might be doing,' Jacques said as the cage door was unlocked and the cold upper air rushed in.

The stitched-faced man loomed tall in front of them. He ushered them out of the mine cage with a grunt, and led them through the cold dusk back to their dungeon cells.

Chapter 17

A WHOLE HEAP OF GOLD
THE SPINNING FACTORY
7 A.M. SHARP

Early the next morning, Ormestone, two of his strong henchmen (with some sacks draped over their arms), and also a pair of fierce wolves, walked briskly from the dark castle through the dark woods to the old palace building. Ormestone was delighted at the way things had gone so far. He had spoiled the big Trueheart wedding, and he had captured all the Trueheart brothers; well, the ones that really counted anyway. The missing bumpkin, so-called 'simple' Jack, would be caught soon enough. He had taken their ridiculous princess brides and he had well and truly spoiled their pathetic happy ending.

There was, of course, that younger one, that awful boy Tom. Reports had come in from the sentinels that he had been seen. Steps were in hand to make sure of him too. Proclamations had already been put up overnight by sprites all over the kingdom offering very tempting rewards of wish fulfilment, something that had been banned outright. Surely that was a big enough prize to tempt any of the pathetic cowed populace to hand Tom in. He wasn't exactly dangerous after all; Ormestone had shrunk him down to the size of a thumb.

Let him try something brave and foolish at that pathetic size. Now there was another stolen story start that had come in *very* useful; I'd like to see him even manage to do anything at all, Ormestone thought. He had not forgotten, nor forgiven, the waste of all that lovely sprite gold that Tom Trueheart had caused him to lose. Whole sackfuls of it had been thrown away out of the old flying machine. He had had to treat it as just so much ballast, in order to survive at all, and some of it was never seen again. Ormestone, however, knew that he couldn't have ended up in a better place than this. It was a place with trolls, goblins, renegade sprites, and other dark forces of all kinds and, above all, old gold mines. He was all set. Now he just had to increase his gold stocks, and by a huge amount. The terrifying general of the Army of Darkness had struck a deal with him, and Ormestone needed an exact amount of sprite gold to pay them. Those so-called adventurers had better work hard in the mine, and the princesses had better have worked their particular magic too.

He unlocked the padlock on the palace door. He petted the guard wolf, and then he climbed the gloomy staircase up to the minstrel's gallery. There was no sign of the princesses, but their spinning wheels stood together in a neat green line, all five, and in front of each was a heap of fresh shining sprite gold.

Ormestone could not believe his eyes.

He went to the first pile and picked up one of the perfect gold ingots. It was so bright it almost hurt his eyes. It was an almost white gold, and pure sprite.

'My my,' he whispered to himself, dazzled.

The doors of the bedchamber opened and one by one each of the princesses filed in wearing their specially provided work clothes. Princess Zinnia pushed back all the shutters on the line of tall windows. The mound of straw had indeed gone down; it was definitely much smaller. When Ormestone looked at it again, the gold looked almost too bright and dazzling in the daylight. The princesses lined up quietly beside their spinning wheels.

'Well, well, well, my fine young ladies, I will admit something to you. I am impressed, and that rarely happens. I see that you have performed very well so far in your task, you really can spin straw into gold. This is good work and a good start. Where, by the way, is my personal sprite?'

'If you mean that horrible little creature with the bent back and the bent stick,' said Princess Zinnia, 'he is in the scullery clearing away our breakfast things. May I say that I saw a rat in there, a big nasty grey rat and it was hard to tell the difference between them side by side.'

'Send him out here at once,' Ormestone said. 'The sprite, I mean, not the rat.'

The little sprite appeared, still wiping at a wooden breakfast bowl with a cloth.

'Good morning, master,' he said, and bowed. Then he saw the dazzling gold and he dropped the bowl on to the ground in shock, where it made a huge clatter. The sprite, too, stared in disbelief at the piles of bright gold ingots laid out beside each of the spinning wheels across the room.

'Marvellous, isn't it. Perfect ingots of sprite gold,' Ormestone said. 'I am so pleased and even, I admit, very surprised that they have managed such a task at all. Perhaps there is more to the magic of the Land of Stories than meets the eye?' he added.

The little sprite looked back at his master and nodded.

'In any case, the result is what matters, but watch them very carefully, and see that they work even harder still. There is more straw to spin before tomorrow, and then a whole new batch of straw may have to be freshly delivered, for more transformations. We shall see. Work well.' With that Ormestone turned to his two henchmen. 'Put all the gold in the sacks, carefully now, and then bring it over to the castle.'

Ormestone slipped back down the staircase with his wolves and left the palace. The henchmen filled the sacks full of gold, and humped them over their shoulders, and then they too clanked their way down the staircase, turning the big key in the lock as they left.

Ormestone paused as he crossed the strange garden, his mind full of the wonder of the perfect gold that the princesses had spun from straw. He found he was looking into the pumpkin face of the scarecrow guard that waited so patiently every day. He came to and saluted the scarecrow, but it failed to salute him in return. Ormestone stood looking at it for a moment.

'What should you have done then in response to my salute, my orange-headed friend?'

'So sorry, your majesty,' said the scarecrow mushily through its grinning mouth, and then it saluted crisply, with its skinny stick of an arm raised to its forehead, the gloved palm open, with the thumb bent inwards.

'Better,' said Ormestone, 'and don't forget ever again. I am your king, after all, and you must always pay me the respect of a salute under all circumstances.'

'Yes, sorry, of course, your majesty,' it said wetly.

'Well, my lovely ladies,' said the sprite after the door had closed on them, 'it seems that the king is very pleased with your "spinning" work', and he chuckled. 'I will order you such a nice treat from the kitchens below.'

'He is no king,' said Sleeping Beauty. 'My father is a king, that man is just a horrible fraud.'

'He is our king,' said the sprite with a trace of sadness, and of regret, in his voice, 'and I have deceived him. I have risked a great deal for all you ladies in making that gold. I am afraid I shall expect some sort of reward, for that is how stories like this always work.' He smiled a little to himself. He picked up a handful of leftover stems of straw from the floor, pointed his little bent stick at them, and instant gold dust sparked and fluttered from his hands.

'You will get a reward, a big reward, we promise you,' said Snow White.

'Promises, promises butter no parsnips,' the sprite said, shaking his head. 'Remind me,' he added slyly, 'are any of you beautiful princesses yet married?'

'You know that we are all betrothed, you should not need reminding of that,' said Princess Zinnia.

'Oh yes,' said the sprite, 'how very silly of me, of course. Those weddings never took place, did they, I remember now. I tell you what, in that case you must all promise to marry me instead, every one of you, before I spin any more gold out of that straw.'

'Marry you?' they cried out as one.

'Yes, I said marry me. Is that such a bad thing?' said the sad little sprite, doing his best to smile.

The girls were struck speechless by the very idea. They stood in a line looking at the little sprite as he petted the remaining guard wolf. The sprite looked up at them.

'I will give you some time to consider my proposal,' he said quietly. 'I will work on this last batch of straw here and while I do you must all think very carefully, and before I finish you must give me your answers. I think you know what will happen if it is the *wrong* answer, for I have the ear of our beloved king, and oh, how he loves his gold, and oh, how he hates to be disappointed.' He pointed the little wand stick at the fragments of gold that he had just made a second or so ago and they turned back at once into drab straw which he kicked aside with his little boot.

The princesses knew now that they had little choice. To survive they must agree to anything he asked, just to keep any hope of escape and rescue alive.

Chapter 18

Tom sat up close beside the woodcutter as they trundled under the dense trees of the dark forest. A few flakes of snow fell around them but mostly they were caught in the overhead canopy, the deep dark tangle of high branches above the road.

'What brought a little lad like you all the way to the Vale of Woodcutters—sorry, to the Land of Dark Stories?' said the old man from the back of the cart.

'I already told you,' Tom shouted back to him, 'I'm here to rescue my brothers and their princess brides, and to prevent our lands being invaded by the Army of Darkness.'

'Big task for a little shrimp like you; are your brothers all the same size as you?'

'No, they are more or less your size; well, my brothers are taller,' Tom added. 'They are adventurers, you see, just as I will be when I am older.'

'Seems to me that the days of adventure are sadly over now,' said the woodcutter. 'Since the Vale of Woodcutters was invaded and he came to rule us here, there has been a change of policy on all our stories. First thing he did was the king put a ban on wish fulfilment and we have wished so hard over the years for a boy of our own. I was talking about it only the other day, wasn't I, dear?'

'Yes, you were, dear,' said the man, 'and dangerous talk it was too, in these times. Well, since *he* arrived.'

'He?' said Tom.

'Our king, the blessed Ormestone,' said the woodcutter, shaking her head.

'Ssh, now,' said her husband.

'King?' Tom shouted in disbelief. 'King? He's not a king, he's just a scribe, a deviser of stories gone over to the bad.'

'That's enough of that dangerous talk,' said the man. 'You'll get us into terrible trouble and I'm armed, you know. I've a valuable old duelling pistol right here in my bag, and if necessary I'll use it; you've been warned.'

'Calm down now, dear. It's all true. Though,' said the woodcutter, 'that's not why we brought along our pistol. The byways aren't safe any more, you see; wolves prowling and much worse. We are meant to report anything of a "magic" nature, and unfairly for us, you are our wish fulfilment. Of course, our stories weren't always dark, mind you, but they were often wintry, and could be spooky and sometimes scary too, and to be fair there were a great many wild animals in them and our tales sometimes ended unhappily. Why, we've supplied woodcutters for all the major stories going right back. Now look around you: it's nearly always winter here. In the olden days there was a little bit of autumn now and then, even the odd summertime corn ritual or two, but now it's just the one season.'

She shook her head and added, 'You're much smaller than we would have liked.'

Then her husband chipped in. 'But you could still have helped us in our work, and being so small you could sneak into tiny places, and lie in wait and thwart any possible robbers and the like,' he added mournfully, thinking of future stories in which their bold brave son, dashing young Tom Thumb, would have featured as the tiny but useful hero.

They trotted on towards a distant clearing. Tom could see a space ahead through the trees. The road they were on was suddenly crossed by another wider road, and there in the middle, on a patch of frosted grass, stood a tall crossroads sign. Tom could see its blank wooden hands pointing in four different directions. Tom could also see, sitting on the finial at the top of the sign, a familiar-looking big black crow. His spirits rose at once.

Tom saw his chance. He got to his feet as fast as he could. 'You mean to betray me then?' he said.

'Sorry, my little man,' said the woodcutter, 'but I fear we have no choice, rules are rules, and we have to hand

you in. I don't want to, but a proclamation is a proclamation, after all, and we have seen what happens to
people who disobey the king. Now just you sit down.'

All the while Tom had been inching away and
beyond the possible reach of the woodcutter. Now he
saw that he would soon run out of space. The woodcutter suddenly turned in her seat and let go of one
half of the reins, leaned across the board and made a
grab for little Tom. The woodcutter's hand almost got
him; below Tom was the hard roadway, and in front
of him was the back of the horse with its swishing tail.
The horse seemed to be moving faster now. They were
rattling on at a good pace towards the crossroads sign.
Tom had to make a decision, and soon: should he go
downwards or forwards? He made up his mind. He
leapt forwards, and landed awkwardly on the horse's
rear end. He stood balanced for a moment just above
the tail, which swished to and fro, threatening to
dislodge him, then he ran along the horse's back,
jumping up on to the bridle and then along its neck.

The woodcutter stood up on the board. 'Come back
here,' she cried, and cracked the reins, which made
the horse move even faster. Tom had to balance care-

fully as he made his way up the mane because the horse was almost galloping now. He turned to look back for a moment, and the woodcutter called out to him again.

'Come back, my little man, come back right now.'

Tom stopped just near enough to the horse's ear, and then he stepped in. It was hot inside the ear, but Tom was able to whisper to the horse, even though he had no idea if the horse understood him or not.

'Keep steady, and keep going as you are. I'm going to go back across your mane and do what I must do. Don't be alarmed by anything, for I mean you no ill. I am Tom Trueheart of the adventuring Truehearts; perhaps you could give me a sign if you have understood me at all?'

Tom climbed out of the horse's hot sticky ear, back into the rush of cold air. The horse gave a loud whinnying sound; Tom hoped that it was the sign that he needed. He turned and started to make his way back down the horse's mane, but it was too difficult and he slipped and fell. He just managed to grip on to the coarse hair of the mane while he swung free over the rushing roadway. His legs kicked out to the side, his body twisting over and over in the onrush of wind. Finally he managed to haul himself up again. In the air suddenly, above the cart, was the crow, which had taken off from the crossroads sign, and was now circling high above them.

Tom steadied himself just above the place where the reins joined the bridle. The horse was certainly running at a steady pace now. Then he heard a familiar voice.

'Whoa there, whoa,' and the horse suddenly slowed and skidded to a halt.

The woodcutter fell over on the driving board, her big boots waving in the air. The old man was spilled out of the back of the cart and landed on his bottom in the road. Tom just managed to hold on. He turned round, and saw none other than his brother Jack standing four square, broad and beefy, holding on to the horse's bridle, in the middle of the road. Jack had obviously slowed the horse right down to a halt with his strength. Tom had never been more pleased to see anyone. He shouted out, 'Jack!' and ran forward down the horse's back, but Jack had not seen him yet. Jack had no idea that Tom was now so small, after all. Tom made it as far as the mane and was about to call out again, when he found himself suddenly lifted up very fast into the air: a set of claws had plucked him straight off the horse's back. He looked up and saw that the crow from the signpost had got him firmly in its grip.

'Jollity,' he called, 'thank goodness. Look, there's our Jack down there.'

'The woodcutter's husband had pulled a pistol out and was about to shoot you, Tom,' said Jollity. 'So I thought it best to lift you out of harm's way.' And so they flew on together over the trees, and after a few moments they heard the loud bang of the duelling pistol being fired.

Chapter 19

Jack had made good progress through the forest. He strode bravely ahead, constantly scanning the road, and sometimes watching his back for wolves or other danger.

He crossed a stout wooden bridge over a wide river, beautifully built and carved from forest oak. Skilled work here, Jack thought. It's very mysterious, but I haven't seen another person since I escaped. Jack looked nervously behind the nearest tree as if expecting someone to pop out suddenly. Maybe they are all in hiding, he thought, or they all blend in so well it's hard to see them, being forest folk, but I don't get a sense of it.

He came upon a sign which proclaimed, 'The Vale of Woodcutters', but the letters were all crossed out with a streak of thick black paint, and beyond was a pile of neatly trimmed logs and trimmed tree lengths piled up beside the road.

Now then, thought Jack, something's up here. No wonder I see the careful work of good skilled wood-cutters, I am in the Vale of Woodcutters. They must have been taken over by the dark forces.

Later he reached a crossroads. The pointing hands were blank, all pasted over with black paper as if no one was actually expected to find the way to anywhere. Below the pointers was nailed a paper notice. 'Hello, what's all this?' Jack stepped off the road on to the central grassy knoll and looked carefully at the notice. It was a big sheet of Story Bureau paper. It had a deep black border all around it, and at the top was a grinning skull and cross-bones, all printed in glossy black ink.

'Well, well,' said Jack reading the notice, 'they work fast, I'll give them that.'

By Order, Big Reward offered.
WANTED

for various crimes including unlawful trespass, wish fulfilment, and seeking a happy ending, two persons answering to the following descriptions:

1. *Jack Trueheart, 20 years old approx., a so-called adventurer. In person a scruffy vagrant, and the answer to at least one wish fulfilment, and most definitely seeking a happy ending for others. He is possibly armed and definitely dangerous. When he was last seen in the great forest, the accused was wearing seven-league boots, tattered green hose, a patched archer's style leather jerkin, and a dirty brown leather weskit.*

2. *Tom Trueheart, twelve years old, brother to the older Jack Trueheart. A gold thief, unlawful trespasser, and vagrant, also the subject of at least one wish fulfilment, and in danger of procuring a happy ending for others, in violation of Rule Seven. Distinguishing marks: is currently the size of the average human male thumb.*

If either or both these wanted persons is seen then they must be reported immediately. Failure to do so will result in the severest possible penalty. You have been warned. The reward offered is exceptional; the rare and forbidden fulfilment of at least one wish! Signed: King J. Ormestone the 1st.

'Scruffy,' said Jack out loud, 'scruffy; the nerve of it. This is rogue sprite work all right; how would they have got these proclamations up so quick otherwise. After all, I only absconded last night.'

Jack read it through again. 'Hold on,' he said, 'what's this bit here about our Tom? Says here he is the "size of the average male thumb". He must be under an enchantment then, poor young lad. That Ormestone, he makes my blood boil, he really does, the swine.'

Jack saw that a rough woodcutter's horse and cart was trundling fast down the road towards him. He went to step back into the road, and as he did so a crow flew off from the signpost finial above him.

Jack could see that the cart driver, a tall peasant woman, was only holding the reins with one hand, while she was trying wildly to snatch at something with the other, and calling out. An old man sat in the back of the cart fumbling with what looked like a big dangerous-looking duelling pistol. Jack set out to halt the out-of-control runaway horse at once. After all, this was surely just the sort of thing adventurers were meant to do, indeed were born for. He jumped out and stood in the road and as the horse passed by he grabbed hold of the bridle.

The horse shuddered and skidded to a dramatic halt, dragging Jack along with it, as Jack in turn dug his seven-league boot heels in hard against the road. They all came to a halt. Jack gave the horse a friendly whack on the flank, and the man tumbled out of the cart onto his behind on the road, and the woman sprawled flat on the driving board.

Jack let go the horse, which turned and watched him, and helped the old man to his feet. 'Why, thank you, young man,' the woodcutter's husband said, carefully lowering his pistol and brushing himself down. Then Jack helped the woman up.

'Are you all right, missus?' he asked.

'Oh yes, thank you, what a brave young man, to step in like that, but is my little boy all right?'

'I didn't see a little boy, missus,' said Jack, looking under the wheels of the cart. 'No one nor nothing under the wheels, I'm glad to say.' He straightened up with a smile and looked into the bushes. 'No, there's no one in there either, missus.'

The old man wandered over to the signpost and sat down and shook his head. Then after a moment he looked up and started reading the notice on the support pole. Then he turned and looked at Jack. Then he got up, crossed over to his wife, and pulled her over to one side.

'I knew it, dear, what did I say all along,' he whispered. 'I've just read that new proclamation over there. It's a wanted poster, describes this fellow here to a T. Not only that but it mentions that little lad we found, as well. Turns out they are both renegades, trespassers, and wish fulfilments on the run, both of them. If we hand them all in we would surely get a big reward,' he said, turning to look across at Jack.

'What reward exactly?' asked his wife, the woodcutter.

'One whole wish fulfilled,' her husband whispered. 'It's on the notice over there, signed by the king and all.' Her eyes lit up, and she raised her hand to her mouth to stop herself calling out in excitement.

Jack was thinking to himself, She said a little boy, little, and there's no sign of 'im. Why, it might have been our Tom.

The woodcutter and her husband were still looking over at Jack suspiciously. Jack went over to them.

'This lad you say was with you in the cart, missus, a small boy, you say; was he small or was he very small?'

'Oh, he was very, very small,' said the woodcutter, making a show of Tom's size by holding her index finger and thumb up, but just a thumb's height apart.

'He was the size of my thumb, maybe a little bit bigger,' she said. 'He was the answer to one of our wishes, or would have been, excepting, of course, that he was so small. Mind you, we were prepared to overlook that,' and she nodded to herself with a little smile, 'until, that is, we found out that he was illegal and wanted,' she paused and then said, 'along of you,' and she nodded sternly. Her husband joined in.

'It's our bounden duty as subjects of King Ormestone to arrest you, and that boy when we find him, and hand you both over to the authorities at once.'

'How did you plan to do that?' said Jack crossly.

'We shall take you to the Dark Castle,' said the man. 'I have my duelling pistol in my hand pointed right at you, don't you worry.'

'Ooh, bless you, I'm not worried. Now, which way is this castle?' Jack said looking up at the blank cross-road signs.

'Why down there, of course,' said the woodcutter impatiently, pointing down the road to the left.

'Then that way lies my adventure,' said Jack, and he strode over to the little cart. 'You shall have this humble cart back and your poor horse too, when I have completed my own story mission,' he said, as he climbed up on to the cart. 'I may be many things, sir, missus, but I can assure you of one thing, I am not a thief.' Jack took up the reins and set the horse off with a click. The horse turned its head and gave a loud triumphant whinny as it trotted off. If Jack hadn't known any better he would have sworn that the horse was smiling.

'You come back here,' shouted the man, waving his antique weapon. 'You'll regret it; it'll be the cartwheel torture for you.' And then he fired the gun, which went off wildly with a great bang and a cloud of choking smoke, knocking the old man back over again onto his bottom.

'Missed,' the woodcutter said. 'I hope you brought some more powder with you?' she added.

'Come on now, my fine looking horse,' said Jack. 'Let's be off with you to the Dark Castle, and as fast as you like.' And the horse galloped away at a lick leaving the woodcutter and her husband to shake their fists after them.

Chapter 20

'Welcome aboard, Tom,' said the familiar and friendly voice, 'and hold on tight.'

They flew around for a little while, too high to see the road below them clearly. They heard a great bang from below and Jollity flew lower. It was then that they saw the wagon again and also that Jack was driving it, and that there was no sign of the woodcutter and her husband.

'Looks like Jack got rid of them,' said Jollity. 'I thought he was about to shoot that gun of his off at you. That's why I couldn't risk leaving you there. Anyway, hold on, Tom, we'll follow Jack for a while until he reaches a good stopping place.'

They flew on as Jack put some distance between him and the woodcutter and her husband. Then after a while Jack slowed the horse to a halt, and Jollity the crow swooped down towards the ground, where Tom could see Jack tethering the horse and cart by the road.

The crow settled on the top of the cart. Jack turned and looked at the bird that had so suddenly landed and perched on the cart.

'One of those awful sentinel birds again,' he said and raised his bow and slipped an arrow against the string. 'This arrow has a crow feather flight; it seems only fair to send it right back to you,' he added with a grim laugh.

'Don't shoot, Jack please,' Tom called out as loudly as he could. 'It's us, it's Tom and Jollity the crow.'

Jack stared at the bird. 'Oh, trying to talk your way out of it now as well, eh.' He stretched out the tight string and took aim.

'No,' Tom shouted as loudly as he could manage.

'Do you know, Jack, I really do think you should wait *just* a little moment,' said Jollity. 'Tom is small, very small, and he's standing beside me right now. Come over and have a look.'

Jack lowered the bow and looked a little closer. He stared down in amazement. The crow was right. There was a very tiny boy, and when he looked really closely he could see that it was indeed his own brother, Tom. At least, it was a very shrunken down version of Tom. As far as he could see Tom was all correct in every detail, right down to his little leather pouch, his pack-staff, his bow, and his sword and scabbard.

'Tom,' he yelled in excitement, nearly blowing Tom off his feet with his breath. 'My, my, you just had a narrow squeak. I nearly loosed an arrow off at you. So the Wanted poster was right, whatever has happened to you?'

'Well, clearly I'm under an enchantment. One of Ormestone's rogue sprites did it,' said Tom.

The horse made a sad whinnying noise; she understood all about enchantments.

'You remember Jollity,' said Tom, 'my friend the crow, who helped us all in the giant's castle above the clouds that time?'

'Course I do,' said Jack. 'Sorry about the arrow just now, only you know how it is. You're famous now, Tom, and so am I,' he added. 'They've put us both up on a wanted proclamation. It's good luck that we have met up like this; now we need to work out what to do next. Between us three surely we can come up with a plan?'

They talked strategies for a while, not getting very far, and then Jack untied the horse and they set off. Jack rattled the horse and cart even further along the road, as far away from the furious woodcutter and her husband as he could. Off they went along the zigzag road towards the flat plain. They finally charged out of the gloom of the winter forest and started to cross over the even gloomier glowering plain. The trees gave way to grubby looking scrubland, with chunks of sharp rock sticking up, and every so often a few of the cart-wheels set up on poles with their bleached skeletons stretched across them loomed up close to the road.

'That's a nasty sight,' said Jack. 'Shall I tell you something, Tom, this is a terrible place,' he added, shivering.

'You're absolutely right there, Jack,' said Tom. 'And to think that our brothers, and their princess brides, are here somewhere in this awful place. We still haven't thought through what to do about it though,' Tom called loudly over the fast rattling of the cartwheels, and the thudding of the poor horse's hooves.

'To tell you the truth, Tom, I must admit that I have no plans at all,' said Jack. 'I'll just hope we think of something when we get there, wherever there is.'

The snow fell steadily now all across the dull grey plain as they raced along the bleak road. After a while they reached the edges of an even darker forest. The horse slowed to an amble, and finally stopped, and stood shivering and steaming under the trees.

'Giddy up, then, old thing,' said Jack, not unkindly.

The horse turned its head in the shaft, and looked at Jack with its big, soft, almost pretty eyes.

'Do you know, Jack, I think that horse is hungry,' said Tom, 'poor thing.'

Jack got down from the cart. He went up to the horse and offered it some scraps from his bag. He was feeling a bit peckish himself, and he was about to mention it when they heard a strange noise from above. It was a single sentinel crow calling out harshly above them.

'How about a crow pie?' Jack asked.

'Good idea,' said Jollity. 'Those are Ormestone's sentinel crows; they've been following us and reporting back on everything we do, I should imagine, by the look of it.'

Jack swung his bow from his shoulder and loosed off an arrow. There was the sound of a very distant and tingly explosion. They all looked up into the heavy sky, and saw a black cloud erupt in the gloom, and then evaporate in a series of strange dark sparkles.

'I swear that was a spell being broken,' Tom called out to Jack, 'look up there.'

A figure was drifting down towards them. It was an ugly-looking little sprite, in a winter cloak and black boots. He was hanging under a sort of black cloth umbrella, which was allowing him to fall slowly, and steadily, down towards the ground.

'What on earth?' said Jack.

'I think that it's some kind of device for sailing through the air,' said Tom. 'Works well, too, by the look of it.'

'I don't much like the look of it,' said Jack, 'to be honest, and I certainly don't like the look of that sprite neither.'

'Looks like a minion sprite,' said Jollity. 'Works for the dark side.'

'Never mind all that for now, that nasty looking little creature's getting closer,' said Jack. He selected another arrow from his quiver, and stood ready to fire. Jack was always the fastest and most accurate with the longbow. He took careful aim, not at the sprite itself, but at the strings supporting the sprite under the billowing black cloth. He fired an arrow and it sped upwards and sliced cleanly through one of the support strings.

The sprite shrieked out in alarm.

Jack flicked another arrow out of his quiver, notched it against the string, pulled it taut, aimed, and fired again.

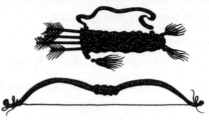

His arrow sliced through another string, and part of the black cloth now flapped upwards, and the sprite shrieked again. He was falling faster now, and tumbling lopsidedly in the air; he would soon hit the ground.

'See, Tom, the forest will provide,' said Jack, pleased with his hand-fashioned weapon and with his accurate work with the arrows.

'What do we do when he reaches the ground though?' said Tom.

'I'm not sure,' said Jack. 'I'll work that out when it happens.'

They watched the sprite as he tumbled down towards them, cursing and shouting and railing at them. The trees broke his fall, and the sprite landed safely enough on the pathway. He tore off the black harness and cloth, and then ran off very fast away from them.

'Well,' said Jack walking over and picking up the circle of black cloth which had a skull and crossbones pattern on it, 'this thing might come in useful, you never know.' He bundled the cloth up and stuffed it in his adventurer's bag, along with the harness and straps. 'They'll know we're coming for sure now,' Jack said looking through the trees towards the horizon.

'We'd best be on our guard then,' said Tom quietly, 'anything could happen.'

They set up camp a little way back from the road among the scant shelter of the trees. They fed and watered the tired horse and then sat around a hastily made fire, and even managed to make a convivial meal of sorts from all their scraps and snow melt. They discussed the rescue options that they thought might be open to them. They tried to make plans using the tiny charts and maps which were in Tom's bundle, although they had to take Tom's word for the chosen route to the Dark Castle, for only Tom could see all the detail on the map.

Jack said, 'We can only hope for the best, for inspiration to come at the right moment when it really matters.'

Tom said, 'The trouble is, we are so used to starting things off after a nice helpful letter from the Story Bureau, and now here we are, all on our own and having to make it up as we go along.'

In the end, after much head shaking, and talking until it was dark, and getting nowhere much, it was agreed that they should travel together for a while and then separate into two teams. Tom and the crow would fly on ahead and try and find the princesses. Jack would take the horse and cart and try to find Jackson, Jake, Jackie, Jacques, and Jacquot, and both groups would try and manage a rescue mission, as best they could, from wherever the Truehearts or the princesses might be being held.

Their hearts were still full of hope, and they bade each other goodnight bravely enough, but Tom's head was teeming with imagined fears of all kinds. As they slept huddled together around the woodcutter's wagon, both of the brave adventurers dreamed in their various ways about the dangerous plains and the cold dark forests of the Land of Dark Stories and what was to come.

Chapter 21

A Night Time Meeting
The Dark Castle
10.27 P.M.

The enormous central tower of the Dark Castle stretched up as high as the lowest of the snow-clouds. Inside, the staircases spiralled up and down and around the curved walls and beyond, and in the castle proper there was a maze of corridors. They led off on every side from the main staircases. Each floor was signalled and crossed by a system of narrow stone bridges supported by buttresses which were often suspended on huge rusted chains, and among the chain links there lived huge, pale, bloated spiders which spun their webs and set their traps.

The castle had stood for as long as anyone could

remember, and no one now knew who had built it. It was surely designed to trap the unwary, and doom anyone foolish enough to enter it. Many of the corridors twisted round on themselves, and many a traveller, hopelessly trying to find a way out, would open a door and step not into a room, but straight out into the darkness of the deep abyss around the tower, or perhaps find themselves walking along a treacherous narrow bridge that stopped suddenly in mid-air.

At the far end of one central corridor was a locked room. In the room, which was lit only by a single guttering candle, sat a friendly-faced man. He was surrounded by stacks of old books and he stopped his reading to write occasionally using a pen dipped in white ink. He wrote notes and figures on a sheet of black paper. In front of him all across the table were a series of glass jars and retorts, mixing bowls, pestles, and scatterings of notes, and many jars of oddly coloured substances. He was tired. His life had passed for a long time now simply working on futile experiments in this room. He yawned and rubbed his eyes, and then he took the metal-framed spectacles from his face and wiped the lenses on a little piece of cotton cloth. The cloth was worn thin with use but close to, in the light of the candle, a very faded pattern could just be seen, a pattern of heart shapes, in almost invisibly pale pink on a dirty white background. He sighed, replaced his spectacles, and tucked the precious little square of cloth back into his pocket.

The corridor beyond the door turned endlessly in on itself like the spiral inside a snail's shell, and at the very end of it was Ending Hall. A vicious fire was blazing, with intense crackling blue flames, while Brother Julius Ormestone, story deviser, self-appointed King of the Land of Dark Stories, and collector of beautiful sprite gold, sat on his black throne musing on his success and counting out his ingots, the lovely pile of pale gold slabs that the princesses had spun from a big heap of humble straw.

He had stolen a whole sackful of story ideas from the Story Bureau. Well, it would be fairer to say that his sprite helper had stolen them. His sprite helper was really the key to Ormestone's kingship. The sprite was the magic power behind the throne, and behind his plans. Ormestone had freely adapted one of the stolen story starts for the princesses. The idea of spinning straw into gold appealed to Ormestone, both as a cruel trick, and as a possible likely source for his favourite substance, sprite gold.

The table in front of him was weighed down with the gold now, so much so that the table actually dipped a little in the middle. The blue flames of the fire reflected across the surface of the gold in startling greenish ripples. Ormestone knew his sprite well, but by no means all of his abilities. He was sure that there were other powers which went much further than the sprite would ever admit to him. Ormestone knew that there was a secret sprite rule which prevented them from making gold directly to order. He also knew something else: he had a dark suspicion as to how the ingots had been made, but for now, well, he would happily bide his time and just encourage things along.

The little sprite himself slipped quietly in through the tall door. He carried his little wand, and he wore a circlet of dead leaves on his head. He looked like a normal everyday green wood sprite that had suddenly suffered the effect of a snap autumn, a season which was, after all, an unhappy ending for leaves.

174

'Ah, there you are, my friend,' said Ormestone. 'Join me.'

The sprite bowed to Ormestone and then hopped up on to a chair near the table. 'Your majesty is pleased and impressed with the gold, I trust?'

'Why, I certainly am. Just look at it all here, piled up in beauty.'

'It does not look so beautiful to me,' said the sprite.

Ormestone looked up sharply. 'What in all the Land of Dark Stories could be *more* beautiful than sprite gold?' he asked.

'Oh, I can think of four or five other things,' said the sprite gazing absently into the blue flames of the fire.

'I don't know what you mean,' said Ormestone, and he reached forward and lifted one of the heavy ingots and weighed it happily in his palm. 'Why, when my beautiful gold harvest is complete, I will have gathered enough in the castle coffers to seal the special bargain and buy the services of all those dark villains and mercenaries travelling here even now from the west. There will be enough for the whole Army of Darkness too, and perhaps even some left over for me.' He chuckled to himself and stroked the softly glowing bar of gold as if it were some favourite pet. He turned to the sprite and continued, 'Those Trueheart men will soon be totally exhausted, ruined even, and I trust utterly useless, after digging out the last of the seams down in the goblin gold mine. Who will there be left to stop me after that? No one, just a half-witted yokel, and a boy the size of a thumb. I don't think they are any threat, do you?'

The sprite gazed dreamily into the blue flames. The intense colour of the fire reminded him of a particular pair of blue eyes, and he sighed under his breath. Something had happened inside his normally flint-hard heart. It was something he had never expected in all his years in the story-making world. Among all the transforming and enchanting something very exciting and terrifying at the same time had happened. He had fallen in love. What's more, he had fallen in love five times over.

His dream, his wish, was to marry all the princesses, and he knew that this was a dream which would be very much forbidden under the rules of his new king and master. It was bad enough that he was transforming straw into gold, let alone having romantic dreams and wishes. There was to be only misery for all and unhappy endings. He could not even hint to Ormestone at the strong secret emotion coursing through his veins. His only hope was to continue his outward professions of disgust, and make Ormestone realize that the worst and unhappiest ending of all would be to let *him* marry all the princesses at once. He smiled just a little to himself, he congratulated himself, but he would have to be very, very careful, and give nothing away, especially to King Ormestone.

The door banged open and a minion sprite ran into the room. He was covered in sprinklings of sooty black dust which flew off him in little swirls as he approached the table.

Ormestone looked up, and frowned; he laid his gold bar carefully back on the table.

'What is the meaning of this?' he asked.

'Forgive . . . huff, huff . . . me . . . huff . . . your . . . huff, huff . . . majesty,' said the sprite, barely able to speak through the gasps and gulps of breath that he was forced to take. He had just run a very long way indeed and was near to collapse.

'You are a king's minion sprite, are you not?' said Ormestone. 'Surely the last time I saw you, you were under an enchantment as a sentinel crow, like most of the others?'

'Yes . . . huff . . . sir, I was indeed, and proud to say I was the squadron leader of B wing attack.'

'What happened to you?'

'I had followed two intruders, the ones you told us to watch for. One of them fired an arrow at me. It must have had enchanted feather flights because it reversed my spell and I fell to earth and ran off to report and here I am.'

The sprite stood with his hands on his knees, catching his breath. Ormestone shook his head.

'You are sure that there were two of these intruders? Was one of them a very, very small boy?'

'Yes, your majesty.'

'It's confirmed then, both of them: the bumpkin adventurer and that boy Tom Trueheart,' said Ormestone.

'Ah, yes, the one that I shrank down for you so easily, majesty,' said the assistant sprite.

'Yes, I am fully aware of who it is,' said Ormestone. 'You have, I hope, already issued the proclamations, describing the tiny boy and the older idiot Trueheart, and have issued all the notices and penalties and possible rewards?'

'Of course, your majesty,' said the minion sprite. 'They are up all over the kingdom, on every village green, most trees, and every signpost.'

'Then it will not be long before someone out there among the low peasantry will be only too glad to report the whereabouts of our adventuring intruders, and claim the one wish fulfilment that is theirs as reward. I must double the special guard on the room along the corridor; you know what I mean by that?'

'Of course, master,' said his familiar sprite.

'By the way, aren't you neglecting your duty just here, my friend?' said Ormestone, pointing to the dusty, sooty, minion sprite, still catching his breath in front of them.

'Of course, your highness, many apologies,' said the assistant sprite. He quickly raised his stick and pointed it at the dusty sprite, who shivered and looked fearful. The poor sprite was suddenly covered in flickers of livid white light; then there was a gathering of darkness at the centre and after the light dispersed there he stood: a crow once more.

'Go then,' said Ormestone, 'fly back to your squadron, back to the murder of crows, patrol the dark skies and don't fail me.'

The crow nodded as if to say 'Yes', and then flew up to the high window ledge. The sprite pointed his little stick at the window and it swung open with a flash of glitter. The crow flew out through the gap with a loud caw and vanished into the night sky.

'You'd best go back to the palace,' said Ormestone. 'See what progress the princesses are making.'

'May I increase their rations a little, your highness, perhaps a nice special sweet cake to celebrate; they have deserved that at least with all their hard work?'

'I hope you are not going *soft* on them, my little friend.'

'No, indeed, your highness,' said the sprite, 'of course not, quite the opposite. I have made them such a cruel offer—' and he stopped himself.

Ormestone looked across at him, from under lowered brows. 'An offer, what do you mean, an offer?' Ormestone asked, his voice as cold as ice.

The sprite panicked. His eyes darted to the heap of gold ingots rippling in the light from the fire, and then darted to the high window, anything to distract Ormestone.

'Well, your majesty, I had thought to include a little extra something in the story, a dark little twist, for the extra pain of the princesses.'

'Oh, have you indeed? Well, never forget,' said Ormestone, 'who exactly the true story deviser is in this room. What pray is this *twist* that you speak of; surely it is up to me to approve of any such matters? Well?'

'I have informed those young women that after their task is finished, they must marry me, all of them.'

'Marry you,' Ormestone said, 'marry you.' He stood up and crossed the few paces between himself and the sprite. He bent close to the sprite's head. He reached a bony hand forward and cupped the sprite's straggly bearded chin, and tilted his head back.

'Look at me,' he said quietly. 'You intend to marry those princesses? Those gossamer fragments of a wish-fulfilling fairy tale, those beautiful maidens, those heartbreaking beauties, love's young dream, and all of them passionately betrothed to one or other of a gaggle of big bold adventurers? And you, my little sharp, twisted, straggle-bearded friend, actually want to marry *all* of them?'

'Yes,' said the little sprite quietly.

'I worry that you *are* going soft on them; in fact, you are plainly soft in the head.'

'No, no, your majesty,' said the little sprite earnestly, 'if anything my attitude has hardened. It will be the perfect *unhappy* ending for them. They have been thoroughly spoiled all their lives and now in the future they will have to wait on me, give in to my every whim. They will have to obey me at all times. They will have to live in my dark, damp draughty little hovel in the woods down the road, far away from the loves of their lives, far from the blue skies and sunshine of the Land of Stories. Be assured that I shall naturally devote my own life to making theirs a total misery.'

Ormestone looked at him carefully.

'I have an idea,' he barked suddenly. 'An extra test, another twist for those ridiculous princesses.' And he dashed across the room and fetched over a sheet of black paper and a bottle of glowing white ink. He sat at the table, smoothed the paper and began to write.

'This is just a little extra insurance, to make doubly sure of their doom. The beauty is that they will never crack it.' He grinned at the sprite. 'You will offer them a tiny glimpse of hope, a release from the thought of this terrible marriage to you, but it will be under one condition and one condition only.'

'A condition, master?' said the sprite, suddenly miserable; worried now that his secret dream was about to be dashed. That he too was to suffer an unhappy ending.

'Yes, a condition, in the form of a riddle, an unanswerable question. You know how they love to include those things in their story planning at the Bureau. We must set something very, very difficult. Now let me see, they must be made to guess something, which will be completely and utterly impossible, and if they don't guess after three attempts, everything must be in threes after all, three wishes, and so on . . . ' He muttered to himself and rummaged in some papers scattered across the table in front of him.

'Ah, here we are,' he held up a piece of paper, 'and here it is, the very thing, embedded like an arrow in the heart of the story itself.' He began to laugh.

'What is it, majesty?'

Ormestone wrote, his hand travelling across the sheet of black paper. He was enjoying the agony and discomfort of his useful nasty-minded sprite. He stopped, squinted at the paper, ran a sifter of blotting sand across it, blew off the surplus, and folded it neatly across the middle.

'There,' he said, 'when the time comes you will read this to them, and that will be that, their misery and their lifetime of unhappiness will be totally assured.'

The sprite looked nervously at the paper. 'Yes, master, your highness,' he said.

'Well read it then; just to yourself, mind.'

The sprite opened the black paper, with a heavy heart. He could not bear to think that there might be a let-out for the princesses. He took a deep breath and he read what Ormestone had written. His face broke into a broad grin. His dream, his most secret wish would most surely be granted now. The king was indeed on his side after all. Later, when he flew back home to his little hut, his dank hovel in the forest, he would start to get it ready for his five lovely wives to move in.

Chapter 22

A Meeting in the Forest
Near Dawn

Jack walked by the horse, Tom rode in the cart, while Jollity flew a little above them keeping a watchful eye out for sentinel crows and the like. They had been travelling since before dawn. Jack seemed strangely restless. It was as if something was in the air that was troubling him. Perhaps it was the faint scent of wood smoke or something else that drifted around them, as if somewhere far away someone was cooking something good, or perhaps he was just anxious to get some practice in with his bow and his arrows. They had worked well so far, and he was keen to get some more shots loosed off before they got anywhere near the looming Dark Castle. Then again something seemed to be calling out to him, a siren voice other than the wood smoke.

Jack patted the horse on the neck and then said to Tom, 'I'm just going off the track for a while. You let the good old horse carry you on along this road and I will find you later.' The horse looked at Jack with her sad dark eyes, but Jack didn't seem to notice.

'You are surely not going away, Jack?' Tom said nervously. 'I can't help thinking that is a very bad idea.'

'Do you now, our Tom?' said Jack.

'Yes I do. We are in the Land of Dark Stories, after all, and that means that almost everything and anyone here might certainly mean to bring us unhappiness, probably harm, and anything that happens will almost definitely lead to a bad ending.'

'I know that, I'm not daft,' said Jack.

The horse turned its head to look at him and gave a low concerned whinny.

'I think that poor horse is fond of you, Jack,' said Tom. 'How shall I protect myself?' Tom added looking around nervously.

'I won't be long,' said Jack. 'You and Jollity can look

out for each other. Why, I'll be back in two shakes of a lamb's tail.'

'It's not the lambs I'm worried about,' said Tom, and as if to back up his fears somewhere in the far distance the cry of a wolf carried on the wind, howling for its breakfast.

'Don't worry about that, that's miles away,' said Jack. 'Just keep to this roadway and I'll find you soon enough.' And with that he set off among the trees.

'Ah, but I do worry,' said Tom to himself as the horse trotted forward down the path, 'I do.' Tom stood up as high as he could on the wagon seat and waved up at Jollity. The bird flew down and landed beside him.

'What is it, Tom?' he said.

'Jack's taken it in his head to wander off on his own. He's left his bow and arrows behind too. Perhaps you could keep an eye on him, see he doesn't get into any mischief.'

'Good idea,' said Jollity, and flew up and after Jack into the forest.

Jack set off through the dark wood on his own and a good feeling came over him for the first time since they had arrived; he suddenly felt like a proper brave adventurer off on a quest. It was not that he wasn't glad to have Tom and Jollity with him, it was just that for now he felt that he must go off on his own; something was compelling him to test his own mettle and have a bit of an explore. This was a mysterious dark wood after all and it was his duty as a story finisher and adventurer to see what was going on, among the dark trees; what made it tick; to discover what adventure was just around the next tree trunk; where that nice smell of cooking was coming from. Perhaps after all he was just hungry for a good breakfast?

He had not gone far when he came to a plain little wooden house. Jollity was flying above him and flew quietly down among the trees and hopped from branch to branch keeping up with Jack, his suspicions aroused. This looked very like a rather neglected sprite house. The house was similar in style but smaller than the

Trueheart house. It was not painted in bright colours, but rather it was the drab natural colour of old weathered timber. The wooden walls were an ash grey colour and the whole house looked broken down and damp and almost haunted, but at the same time, there was a merry welcoming drift of savoury white woodsmoke coming from the little tin chimney. Jack hoped that it might even be the very smoke that he had sensed earlier on the air. It smelt like bacon. Jack was getting hungrier by the minute, and the house looked odd but seemed harmless and almost friendly.

Jack got his first big shock when he got close and peered through the little latticed window. Outside it looked like a humble little wooden house, but inside it looked more like a palace. It seemed somehow much bigger inside than out, and was furnished with what looked like glittering gold furniture and heavy velvet fabrics. The floor appeared to be made of the finest marble, and there was even a wide staircase which swept up between two huge gold mirrors. In fact there were mirrors everywhere.

Jollity flew down near Jack and settled on the windowsill; he peered into the gloomy interior of the cottage.

'Mirrors to reflect true beauty,' he heard a voice say from inside the little house. The ragged curtains at the downstairs window hid some of the interior so that Jollity could not quite see who was speaking. Jack had moved to the next window along and hid himself among the tangled branches that covered the dirty glass.

A little person could be seen sitting on a gold chair in the tiny house. It wore a long dark cloak, with a hood. A fine-looking plate of bacon and eggs sat on the gold table in front of it, but it did not appear to be eating it. It held out its arm with a little twisted stick of wood and pointed at the wall. A great gold-framed mirror suddenly appeared on the wall, and then the figure pushed back the hood of the cloak, to reveal, and here Jack got his second shock, the little sprite who had piloted Ormestone's airship.

A tinkling clock bell sounded from the back of the little cottage.

'Now time for breakfast, I'm thinking,' said the sprite with a beaming smile on his face. Jack stared in at the breakfast sitting on the table. He realized how very hungry he really was. He could stand it no longer. Sprite or not he needed that breakfast. He stood back from the window and reached for his bow and quiver. He discovered he had left them behind with Tom and in his shock he stepped back on to a large dry twig which snapped with the sound of a hunting gun going off. Jollity quickly flew away up onto the sagging porch roof.

'Who's there?' said the sprite out loud, bustling to the door and opening it wide.

Jack stood there momentarily, unarmed, fuddled, and

transfixed with both hunger and horror. The little sprite saw Jack, and Jack saw into the house. He was hardly able to believe what he saw. There were pictures on the walls, and all were in elaborate gold frames. He noticed that each of the paintings was of a beautiful young princess. They were all of his brothers' brides-to-be. The sprite quickly pointed his little wand and a sprite-iron chain and manacles snapped across Jack's arms and ankles. Jack came awake properly for the first time that morning. He had fallen into a trap, and all through his stomach and the smell of bacon.

The little sprite stood with a big grin on his face.

'Oh, I am so glad, the king will be so very pleased that you've joined us after all,' he said. 'Now you can help out in the goblin gold mines; after all why should your brothers do all the work and suffering for you?'

Jack strained against the manacles. 'So this is your horrible little nest in the woods, is it?' he said furiously. 'How dare you have those pictures of my brothers' lovely wives-to-be on your horrible walls?'

'Oh, very well then, here is a simple answer for simple Jack. They are not yet your brothers' wives. If you remember, there was an interruption at the wedding and the wedding never happened. Soon though they will all be my wives, every one of them.'

'You must be mad,' said Jack struggling hard at the manacles.

'I assure you it is true. They owe me a debt of gratitude. I will tell you something else, and here is the secret and really clever part, and only you will know this.' He moved nearer to the flailing figure of Jack. 'If they guess my name they will be free to marry who they choose. The problem for those lovely girls, of course, is that no one knows my name, except the king and me, so they will never guess ever, and they will only get three tries. Three of everything, you see, just as in the Land of Stories.' He laughed again.

'You can stop all that struggling by the way.' The sprite sat down at the table again and attacked his bacon and eggs. 'Excuse me, won't you, while I finish my breakfast.'

Jack watched in agony as the sprite wolfed down the bacon and eggs. When he had finished he pointed his stick at Jack's legs and the chain between the manacles lengthened as more links flew into place.

'Now, a little trip to the gold mines where you

belong, I think. I am sorry that you will have to miss my wedding to your brothers' fiancées.'

The sprite laughed and then shut the door of the little house, turned the key in the lock, and marched Jack through the trees at the point of his wand. They walked only a little way, Jack stumbling and cursing over the chain between his legs until they came to a clearing where a tall wicker basket stood with a big balloon floating above it on a series of ropes.

'I find flying such a quick and easy way, so it's either this or my broomstick. As I have company today this will be best, makes it so much easier to get between the old palace and my little house here where my loves and I shall all live together so happily. Hop in and we shall begin.'

Jollity had followed the sprite and Jack on their short walk through the woods to the balloon. He sat hidden among the dark branches and watched. The sprite followed Jack into the basket and cast off so that the balloon soon rose up and flew past the high branch where Jollity was sitting. The sprite looked at Jollity and Jollity looked back at the sprite as blankly as he could. The little sprite's eyes narrowed; it was almost as if he sensed the presence of another sprite for just a moment. However, they were soon high over the forest and a flock of sentinel crows soon joined them on their short trip to the goblin gold mine.

Jollity knew just what he must do now. He had overheard everything that the little sprite had said. He flew back to the dank little house, landed on the sagging roof, and looked for a way in. He flew down and circled the mysterious and crabby-looking little house. One of the dirty latticed windows was missing some of its diamond-shaped panes at the top. Jollity squeezed his way through the gap. Inside was indeed a shock: the unlikely sumptuous furnishings, the mirrors, the gold-framed pictures; it was a palace in miniature. He had no time to explore. He knew just what he was looking for. He found a little study room off the kitchen. It was dark and cobwebby with creaky bookshelves lined with spell books and the dark walls were covered in framed certificates of all kinds. Jollity flew carefully around the room, reading the various documents, letters, and certificates of magic until he found the one he was looking for. A graduation certification of Sprite Magic made out in the name of . . .

Aha, he thought, there you are; got you, my nasty little friend.

Jollity read the carefully hand-lettered name. It was certainly a very unusual name and he said it over and over a few times in his head. It was very important that he should remember it exactly so that he could tell it to Tom the moment he flew back. After all, the happiness of the Truehearts it seemed now depended on it.

Chapter 23

SOMEWHERE ON THE ROAD TO THE CASTLE
MID-MORNING

Tom sat waiting on the cart for Jack and Jollity to come back, while the nice carthorse munched dreamily at the dry grass. Then Tom saw, to his amazement, a balloon, very like Ormestone's flying machine, suddenly rise up from among the dark trees into the sky. He heard Jack's voice shouting from the basket. The balloon was too far away for Tom to hear exactly what Jack was shouting, but it didn't sound as if he was very happy. The horse lifted her head and gave a loud whinnying noise at the distant sound of Jack's voice.

At that moment Jollity suddenly landed back on the wagon in a state of agitation, flapping his wings, and said straight away to Tom, 'I have something very important to tell you, Tom. This is something you must write down, it's that important; it must not be forgotten. A lot depends on it.'

Tom had scrambled to his feet and pointed to the sky. 'There was a balloon in the sky like the one Ormestone had, and I think Jack was in it.'

'He was,' said Jollity. 'Now, have you got something to write on and to write with?'

'What is all this about?' said Tom.

Jollity explained in a rush about Jack being caught in a trap snooping at the strange house, and being taken off to the goblin gold mine, about the terrible danger the princesses were in, and especially the secret name of the little sprite and what that knowledge meant. Tom rummaged in his bundle; the back of one of the maps was clear paper, and he fished out a little pencil as well.

Jollity spelled out the secret name.

'Are you sure?' said Tom.

'Very sure,' said Jollity.

Tom licked the end of the pencil and wrote the name down very carefully, then he folded the map and stuffed it back into the bundle.

'I'm set,' he said to Jollity.

'Then I think the time has come for us to go now, Tom, and do our best.'

'Wait,' said Tom, 'what about this poor horse and the cart? Jack left his bow and arrows here, we can't just leave them.'

The horse was looking over at Tom and the crow with a very sad expression in her soft eyes.

'We'll be much quicker in the air, and time is of the essence. She'll be safe enough here; there's lots to eat and the bow can look after itself.'

The horse seemed to nod sagely.

'Well, if you are sure,' said Tom.

Tom climbed on to Jollity's back and they flew up into the air and circled the woodcutter's horse and cart once. Tom waved and called down.

'Goodbye, old friend. We'll be back for you, I'm sure.' And then Tom and Jollity flew off.

The horse watched them go, and thought very quietly to herself, And then there was one.

Chapter 24

The Old Palace

Tom and the crow flew straight up, high above the forest, and as they flew the Dark Castle with its huge pointed-topped tower loomed ever larger on the horizon.

'I hope poor Jack can cope wherever he is,' said the crow.

'He will,' Tom yelled back at him over the sound of the rushing air. 'He's very brave and certainly very tough. Anyway it's our job now to find and save the poor princesses.' He shivered, and clutched tight to his bundle with the vital name in it, partly from the cold but mainly from fear of dropping it.

Tom was having fresh doubts about his courage and more especially about the total misery of his size. What would it be like now to confront the dreaded Ormestone, and that evil little sidekick who had so easily trapped Jack? He had no idea if he could do it. He would need all his courage and all his strength in the almost certainly terrible battle to come. How on earth was such a motley army, a boy the size of a thumb, and a crow, and a friendly horse, supposed to ever rescue brides and grooms and stop Ormestone and the Army of Darkness from invading the Land of Stories? The thought terrified him, and somewhere at the back of his mind there lurked his other promise: to find his poor missing father. He sighed into the wind, and pressed himself close to Jollity, just for the simple reassurance of a friend.

The crow flapped his wings harder and flew as high as he could. He had seen and noticed something ahead that Tom could not. With his acute crow vision he had noticed that the dark snowclouds that seemed to surround the tall tower of the castle on the horizon ahead were not actually snowclouds at all, but a swirling cloud of bats and birds, all of them flying in a great mass, to and fro, over and around the sharp pinnacles at the top of the tower. Jollity knew that every beat of his wings was bringing little Tom nearer and nearer to a very real danger.

It was just then that Tom suddenly yelled out to the crow to fly down lower. Tom had been scanning the ground as they flew and he had seen something odd. Something was waving and flapping out of one of the windows of a big square red brick building. There was an odd sort of garden surrounding the building, full of trees which were clipped into strange shapes. It was all enclosed by a high wall and it looked like a palace, a once beautiful palace perhaps, but now, even from a high distance, it looked like a ruin. However, Tom had noticed the flapping white cloth, and as they flew lower and drew nearer to the building he saw that it was just what he had thought it was, a long piece of white silk muslin, like a torn-off section of a wedding train being waved like a distress flag. It seemed then that this could well be the place where the poor princesses were being held captive.

The building was tall and square with deep pointed windows. The crow skimmed around the garden with Tom looking for any clues as to how to get inside or indeed whether the princesses were there at all. At one end of the garden, wreathed in a cold mist, there was a scarecrow. It stood with its arms outstretched, its tattered coat flapping around it, and a battered old hat pulled down tight on its round head.

The crow flew near it. 'Just to show that we aren't scared of any old scarecrow,' he called back to Tom. The crow settled on the top of the scarecrow's hat. Tom looked up at the palace windows. There were three deep ones on the side facing the scarecrow. They had pointed tops like a church window or like the windows in the witch's gingerbread cottage, only these were much bigger and deeper. Tom was certain that this was where he had seen the flicker of movement at the window, and, sure enough, the length of dirty white silk was still being frantically waved up and down.

'Right,' said Tom, 'they're up there, let's go.'

The crow lifted off from the scarecrow's hat; Tom felt the up-rush of air and then with a sudden jerk he fell from the bird's back down the face of the coat and into the scarecrow's pocket. He struggled to his feet and peeped out over the ragged pocket edge. Jollity struggled and flapped his wings but he was held firmly in the gloved hands of the scarecrow, which had simply reached up and grabbed Jollity as he tried to fly. Tom could see the poor bird struggling in the trap, calling out in alarm, while the fingers held firm.

Tom climbed out of the pocket and made his way slowly up the overcoat, using the buttons and creases and folds in the fabric as footholds. He reached the upper front and stood balanced on the reinforced stitching across the top of a breast pocket. Something caught his eye: a little corner of cotton cloth tucked into the pocket. Tom noticed a heart printed on the fragment of cloth— a piece of Trueheart cloth. He was stunned; how had this got there? Another Trueheart had passed this way, and a long time ago. It could only be one person. Tom's heart pounded in his little chest. Had someone left this for him to find, perhaps? He tore off a section of the fragile cloth and put it into his packstaff.

The scarecrow had slowly turned its head to look down, and when Tom looked up he saw that the scarecrow's head was a bright orange pumpkin. The pumpkin had a jagged carved grin slashed across its face and had two narrow slit cuts for eyes. 'Welcome,' it said to Tom, 'to the October country, the Land of Dark Stories.' It had an unearthly voice, wet sounding, mushy and gleeful, as if it couldn't wait to get hold of Tom too, and when it spoke pumpkin seeds sprayed out of its mouth.

'Go on, Tom,' Jollity called out, 'run, go and find them. I will find you whatever happens. Just go now, don't worry about me.'

Tom noticed a loose thread dangling from a button near the pocket. He jumped down and grabbed on to the thread. He hoped it would both hold him, and also spool down far enough so that he could get to the ground fast. The thread unravelled and Tom abseiled down the crumpled front of the old overcoat. He kicked away from the dirty fabric as he travelled down towards the cold ground. The length of thread suddenly ran out, pulled free, simply gave way, and he fell for the last few feet. He managed to grab the edge of the coat, which broke his fall just before he hit the ground. He swung there for a moment looking down. It was hard to judge the distance, but in the end he decided that he had better let go and drop before the scarecrow snagged him too. He fell through the cold mist and landed in a clump of frosty grass. Nothing broken, nothing lost, he picked himself up and scampered off up the pathway towards the old palace building.

He needed to look for a way in. He was anxious about Jollity, but he was also excited about that little piece of Trueheart cloth. He turned and quickly looked back. The scarecrow was walking across the garden still holding on tightly to poor Jollity. Tom ran as fast as he could. The scarecrow could cover more ground than he could, so he had to be quick. He knew that he would have to get up to one of the upper floors where the tall windows were to find whoever it was that had waved the white cloth.

He rushed around the outside edges of the palace, using the narrow pathway between the palace walls and the tall weedy grass. He could still hear the creak and crack of the brittle scarecrow's legs following behind him. He just needed to hide from sight. He remembered one of his brothers once saying that 'cover from view is not necessarily cover from fire, Tom,' but cover from view was all he was after right then. He took his packstaff, pulled out the bundle with the piece of paper with the name written on it and other useful things, and hid the rest behind a shrub near the door. He adjusted his bow and quiver and set off.

Above him to one side was a high window all covered over in steam and condensation. Being small, he soon discovered, did have some advantages after all. It was possible to squeeze into very tiny spaces and find ways into areas that would normally be closed off to him. He was able to inch his way through a gap in a back door that was grown over with a tangle of dead briar stems and thorns.

It was dark on the other side of the door. He could hear loud clattering sounds, the crash of metal on metal, and a man's voice singing very out-of-tune and very loudly, and the song he was singing was, 'Tom, Tom, the piper's son'. This gave Tom a very strange feeling, as if the voice somehow knew he was there, and was singing about him especially.

He crept carefully along the passageway following the sound of the voice. A big door stood half open. Tom peeped around the door and saw into a long busy kitchen. There was big range made of blackened iron, and strings of onion and garlic hung down from the high ceiling. There was a deep sink and a water pump and a long plain wooden table, and on one wall were rows of shelves, laden with copper pans, pots, jelly moulds, and cauldrons, and hundreds of dusty looking cookery books.

A tall red-faced chef in a white hat stood by the table. He was singing his little ditty and hacking at something on a chopping board. A skinny little assistant chef, with an even redder face, was clattering some big pans out of the steaming sink and piling them one on top of the other on a draining board. There was a good fug of steam in the kitchen and also the smell of baking, which made Tom feel hungry. There was a loud whistle and the chef stopped singing and went over to a speaking tube on the wall. He lifted the earpiece and then shouted very loudly for his assistant to be quiet. Tom slipped behind the table leg and listened.

'Very well, yes, of course, oh, certainly, when? At once, goodness me, oh, well, if we must,' and he replaced the earpiece, and turned back to the table.

'His highness the king himself is coming down here right now,' he said. 'He wants us to make a cake for the princesses and we must make it right away, with no please or thank you neither, typical of him, do this, do that, morning, noon, and night.'

'The big boss, the king down here, a cake,' said the assistant chef gabbling in a muddle and a panic. 'Right away . . . now,' and he immediately dropped a large copper simmering pan on to the stone flags of the kitchen floor with an enormous crash.

'Yes, yes,' shouted the chef. 'For goodness' sake leave those now, just make some cake mix, get some flour, and break some eggs into a bowl, and very quietly mind. No more dropping metal things, you've given me a headache.'

'Yes, chef.'

The assistant's feet dashed past very close to Tom and then back again.

He definitely mentioned the king and the princesses, Tom thought, so this really is where they are. He started to climb very slowly up one of the carved wooden legs of the kitchen table. I'd better hide myself, he thought. He inched his way cautiously further up the table leg and tucked himself under the edge of the table. The door crashed open and Tom froze at the sound of a familiar voice.

'Listen to me and listen well. This cake will take the form of a wedding cake: white icing, columns, and on top, five brides and one groom in sugar icing and marzipan. Do you understand?'

'Oh yes, your highness . . . mm . . . er . . . yes, sire,' came the hushed nervous replies.

'When the cake is baked and iced summon help on the speaking device over there, and then you will leave, understood?'

'Oh yes, your majesty, understood.'

'Good.'

Tom pressed himself further against the underside of the table as the figure moved near to him and stopped. He could see Ormestone's cloak.

'My friend and assistant has earned a very special reward. He has captured that great lummox Jack Trueheart, and all by himself too. We shall slice the cake in celebration. The poor princesses will never answer the question; who on earth would guess what his name might be. After all, there can only be one.' And here he lowered his voice, and said the name very quietly but Tom, crouched so close, heard it all right. Jollity had been absolutely right, it was the very name written down on the back of the map tucked safely in his pocket. A name indeed to remember. Once Ormestone had said it he burst out laughing, and Tom even heard the chef and his assistant laughing nervously in the background too. Then the door slammed shut again in an instant and Tom knew he had to get upstairs fast; perhaps if he hid on a tray or under a plate or something he might smuggle himself in with the cake. He eased himself up and peeped over the edge of the table. The assistant chef was now bent over a big china mixing bowl breaking eggs and muttering to the chef.

'He had to come in here, had to make things difficult for us, oh my.'

'Never mind, he's gone now,' the chef said. 'Get on with it; a bit less of the chat and a bit more of that.' And the chef mimed a stirring motion with his big arm.

'How many eggs to make a princess' wedding cake, chef?'

'How should I know?' the chef bellowed. 'Look in the special unhappy recipe book.'

The assistant chef wiped his hands on his apron and ran over to the shelves on the wall. Tom heaved himself up on to the table and while the chef was looking over at his assistant and shaking his head Tom took his chance and dashed across the table top. He dodged between cups, glasses, measuring jars, and wine bottles. There were sticky wooden spoons and sharp knives and cleavers to dodge until he reached the big mixing bowl. He crouched beside it, his heart thumping, and waited well hidden behind a silver sugar sifter which had fancy curled feet.

'Says thirteen eggs here,' the assistant chef called out.

'Thirteen it is then, you clot, obviously, a baker's dozen, and quite right.'

'Yes, chef,' the assistant called back.

Tom heard the eggs cracked one by one; heard the

gloopy sound of the mix being stirred. He had made himself as small as possible. He was crouched down right against the side of the bowl while he looked round for a suitable tray to hide on. The sugar sifter was suddenly lifted up and crashed down again, and as it came down one of the fancy curled silver feet hooked itself around and under Tom's belt. He felt the silver metal suddenly cold against his back. He stood up and struggled to free himself.

The assistant chef said, 'Those princesses will all have a sweet tooth, I'll be bound.'

'Well then, you chump, put in some more sugar,' said the chef.

Tom looked up and to his horror saw the giant hand of the assistant chef come down and pick up the sugar sifter for the second time. Tom was pulled up with it. He dangled in the air from the foot of the sifter, and he found himself looking down into the creamy cake mixture. When he was little, (what was he *now* then? he thought) he would beg to eat any left-over cake mix. He so liked to lick it, when he was allowed, from the sticky wooden spoon and sometimes his mother would ruffle his hair and give in to him. Now he realized that he was about to drown in a whole deep bowl full of nothing but cake mix. He felt his belt slip as the sifter was shaken hard. Tom was shaken free and fell through the air with all the sugar, his cloak billowing out behind him as he plunged into the sweet sticky mixture with a thick splash.

'What on earth was that?' asked the chef.

'What?' said the assistant chef.

'I swear something just fell into that cake mix.'

'No, chef, it couldn't have,' said the assistant. 'I was only putting in some more sugar like you said.'

'It looked just like one of those filthy rats to me.'

'No, surely not a rat, chef; you've been working too hard. We got rid of all the kitchen rats, remember, under orders from him above. You sent them off to live in the princesses' scullery upstairs. You sit down for a minute, take the weight off. Let me just pop this mix in the cake tin and then I'll put it all in the range oven to bake, and after I've done that I'll make you a nice cup of strong sweet tea.'

'Well,' said the chef, 'perhaps I should, if you're sure,' and he sat down heavily on a chair.

Tom was by now deep under the surface of the cake mix. Luckily his cloak had formed a little pocket of trapped air all around him. Suddenly he felt everything being churned around. Then he was lifted up inside the whole mess of cake mixture, and fell again, all muddled up with the mix, into a deep cake tin. He waited, not sure what to do next, as the mixture settled around him, and then suddenly, after a moment or two, without warning, it all started to get very, very hot.

Chapter 25

The balloon touched down near the mine workings. The sprite ordered Jack out of the basket then walked him over to the dark entranceway under the pit-head wheel. The sprite pointed his little wand at the bell which hung high over the doorway. The bell set up a mournful clanging and after a moment one of the goblins appeared. He broke into a grin at the sight of Jack standing chained in front of him.

'He tells the five others that we would soon have the sixth with us, and he is right. When we get down below he gives the sixth a shovel, he gives the sixth a pick, he gives the sixth a lantern, and then the sixth one digs out the gold, oh yes.'

The stitched-faced man appeared, lurching across the scrub land. The goblin opened the cage door and the stitched-faced man grunted and pushed Jack into the cage with him.

The sprite watched as the lift door was locked and then he said, 'I wish I could stay longer but alas I must away. Tell your brothers that I am off now to a special betrothal party where their brides-to-be are to be the brides and I am to be the groom, oh yes, while they are down there working in the darkness. Farewell, Simple Jack.'

Jack tried to grab the cage door but the stitched-faced man started to lower the cage. Jack, undeterred, shouted up at the sprite. 'We'll get out of here and we will come to find you and we will . . . ' but his voice faded away to a whisper.

The sprite went back to his balloon, untied the anchor rope, and set off back to the palace. 'I have a lovely tea party to go to,' he said, straightening his cloak about his shoulders.

Chapter 26

THE OLD PALACE
DRAWING ROOM
TEA TIME

Snow White and Sleeping Beauty sat together in the upper drawing room of the old palace. They were side-by-side on the velvet sofa, and Snow White handed round the delicate best tea cups and saucers from the silver tray to each of the other princess brides, while Beauty poured the tea, and either added a dash of milk, or a slice of lemon according to taste. Ormestone's recently arrived little assistant sprite sat perched on a chair in the middle of them all and watched them, looking very pleased with himself as he basked in their beauty and charm. He was truly happy.

'I've got crumbs all over my dress,' said Rapunzel, 'from those oat biscuits.' And she stood and swept regally over to the tall window. She opened the window, raised her dress a little, and shook the crumbs off her skirt, taking the chance once more to flap some of the white fabric frantically, desperately, out of the window. She had been making the signal as often as she dared; after all, there was a faint chance that someone might see it, and perhaps a daring rescue might follow.

The princesses had been allowed to change into their tattered wedding garb for this occasion, for their special betrothal tea. Each of the princesses in turn had found some excuse to wave lengths of their tattered white silk wedding fabric out of one or other of the high windows as a last desperate signal for help. It did not seem to have done any good.

Rapunzel looked over at the sprite, who sat watching them all. He was sitting on top of a pile of thick books balanced on the seat of a gold chair. He held a tea cup and saucer, and crooked his little finger exactly as if he were some grand courtier taking tea at court, instead of the rough-dressed little snaggle-bearded wood sprite that he was. He had been telling them how he travelled in his flying machine back to his little sprite home in the dark woods every evening and was busy making it a little nicer each time in readiness for their arrival.

There was a knock at the door. 'Come in,' the sprite called out.

The door opened and a flunkey appeared pushing a white iced cake on an elaborate trolley. It was a miniature wedding cake in two halves, one balanced above the other on white sugar columns and on the top layer of icing there stood some little figures all made of coloured marzipan and icing sugar. There were five little princess figures surrounding one little sprite figure in a dark cloak. The flunkey wheeled the cake into the room, followed by King Ormestone himself and one of his growling pet wolves.

'Continue, please, with your *delightful* tea party, my princesses,' Ormestone said, and he went over and shut the half-open window. 'I wouldn't miss this for anything,' he added, 'you deserve a reward, after all that sprite gold you have spun for me. Why soon, what with that and all the gold that your *will never be now* husbands have so carefully mined for me, I will have every last single dot and tiny speck of sprite gold that there is to be had in the Land of Dark Stories, which will be exactly, but exactly, enough for my very dark needs,' and he laughed to himself.

The princesses drank their tea, and exchanged glances with one another; they were dreading what was about to happen. Ormestone stretched and yawned and then sauntered over to the cake and the wolf trotted at his heels.

'Do you see,' he said, 'on the cake here, five lovely little princess brides, and one very eager groom, modelled on my sprite friend and helper here. This, as you can see, is a wedding cake. It was such a shame for you that I interrupted that other wedding of yours, was it not. You would all be married by now, lovely girls such as yourselves *should* be married, but married, I believe, to the right person. This little sprite here is, of course, *just* the right person. He will supply a proper ending to your stories, my sort of ending. It will be the very ending that we demand here in the Land of Dark Stories: an unhappy one. And soon, of course, these kinds of endings will spread, through the actions of my Dark Army of Occupation, across the whole of the

Land of Stories, too, and further, deeper, into the Land of Myths and Legends and beyond, and do you know, there is not a meddling Trueheart in sight to stop me. There is no one here at all to save you from this particular ending. There is nothing now to save you from your fate. One of the brothers escaped.' The princesses looked at each other in shock. 'Yes, escaped boldly from my captivity, but it didn't take long for my sprite friend over there to take him prisoner again. Such a resourceful little fellow; brave, too, to tackle Jack Trueheart like that. Look at him there, your oh-so-keen and eager husband-to-be.' He paused in his waffling, enjoying their discomfort. 'Well, except that there is one *tiny* thing that might just save you from this marriage. The correct answer to a certain question. I shall cut the cake in a moment, but first I just had to mention *the question*. Well, it will be more of a riddle, really. It is my little friend here that will ask it.'

Ormestone bowed to the sprite, who quite suddenly and eagerly stood up on the books piled on the seat of his chair so that he reached to an almost normal height.

'I will soon be marrying all of you, my princesses,' he said, nodding his head up and down very fast. 'It was thought fair, polite even, that you should be given some chance of a choice in the matter,' he added, his head tilted on one side, a fleeting moment of doubt, of worry, suddenly visible on his little face. 'Our gracious king has made a condition, a stipulation, in order to give you all a fair chance.' He paused, and looked from one lovely face to the next, each princess in turn poised in surprised anticipation, holding her delicate china tea cup before her.

'That is that you will answer my one simple question,' the sprite continued. 'And to be even fairer, that you will have three chances to answer it correctly.'

'Three and only three,' Ormestone added. 'Three strikes and you're out. If you have failed to answer correctly you will all be betrothed and married to my friend here on the instant,' he chuckled. 'But first I think that lovely slice of betrothal cake to eat with your tea, and while you eat you can ponder the answer to the question.'

Ormestone pulled the stolen ceremonial sword of the Story Bureau out from under his cloak. 'I knew that this sword would come in useful, more than once, so sharp, and was it not forged, like my other sword, by old Jack the Giant Killer Trueheart himself? And what better implement could there be for cutting such a momentous cake.'

He raised the sword in the air above his head, and then brought it down swiftly but gently towards the top layer of the cake. Each of the princesses watched the sleek silver blade as it split the polite air of the drawing room. Ormestone looked up and grinned his big yellow-toothed grin. 'Oh, unhappy day,' he said, as the sword blade split the little marzipan figure of the sprite on the cake neatly in two.

'Sorry,' Ormestone said to his sprite. 'Not an omen, I hope.'

'Tis no matter, your majesty, it's not me, after all, but only an effigy made of icing sugar and marzipan,' said the sprite nervously, his heart fit to burst with love for the princesses, all of them paused aghast with their tea cups, and his dream, his wish, so nearly fulfilled. Oh please, he thought, please hurry up.

The sword sliced through the cake cleanly to the bottom. Then the sword fell again and again until five neat slices of cake were laid on the five delicate china plates.

'There,' said Ormestone, 'enjoy the cake while you ponder the question, and remember you have only three attempts at an answer.'

The flunkey handed round the plates of cake, one to each of the princesses, and withdrew, clicking the door shut. Then the sprite took a deep breath and pulled a folded piece of black paper from his little pocket, unfolded it, and read out loud:

'By order of his royal highness, our great king Julius Ormestone, of the Land of Dark Stories, I am empowered to ask of you five eligible princesses the following simple question.' There was a sudden hush in the room. The princesses stared open-mouthed at the little sprite, waiting for him to speak again. He enjoyed his moment of power. He waited, and then he quietly read again: 'What is my name?' he said. And then he sat down on the chair.

There was a long silence in the room, only the mantel clock, all covered over as it was in dust and cobwebs, managed to make any sound at all as it ticked and tocked in the desperate quiet.

Tom had spent what seemed a very long time crouched over in the sticky cake mix. He suffered the terrible heat of the range oven as the cake mixture rose and cooked around him. He was soon hemmed in by the cooling cooked cake. He was at least able to eat some of the cake around him and make himself a bigger air pocket. It was a nice cake too. After a while he felt the whole thing suddenly being lifted up. He heard muffled voices. He strained to hear what they said, but it was impossible. It sounded like the chef and his assistant arguing with one another and then Tom just seemed to drift off to sleep in the soft warm sponge of the sweet cake.

The next thing he knew he was woken by a sharp silvery giant sword blade which suddenly plunged into the cake, only just missing him. Then the blade sliced through again on the other side of him so that he was left rolled up inside a single wedge-shaped slice of cake. He felt himself lifted into the air. He heard voices now and they were clear this time. There was no mistaking one dreaded voice: it was Ormestone himself. 'Enjoy the cake,' he said, 'while you ponder the question, and remember only three tries at an answer.'

The moment has come, Tom thought. He snapped to at once. He raised his head from the cowl of his cloak and peeped out of the side of the slice of cake. He could see the lovely Rapunzel up close. His slice of cake was on a china plate in her hand. He could see her face, her clear blue eyes, and her trailing long hair. The answer to this question, clearly vital for all of them, for the princess brides, and, of course, for his brothers too, was written in pencil on the back of his map. Then he heard a voice he had never heard before, a squeaky chilly little voice, which sounded like a hinge that needed oiling. It read out the proclamation ending with the words, 'What is my name?'

There was a long pause. The ticking of the clock. Tom gasped. 'Right,' he whispered to himself, and rummaged carefully in his pocket for the vital piece of paper. He now knew exactly what to do next.

Chapter 27

A Very Unhappy Ending for Someone
The Old Palace
Some moments after tea was served

Tom had memorized the strange name in any case, better safe than sorry. With great care he began to tunnel himself out of the web of sweet cake and on to the smooth plate. He lay still, face down on the plate, and dared to look round the room. All eyes were on a little sprite standing high on a pile of books balanced on a chair. The plate Tom was lying on was balanced too, only it was in one of Rapunzel's fair hands, and a tea cup and saucer were in the other. She was staring straight ahead at the sprite. Tom looked down and saw that there was a deep chasm, a gulf of space that dropped away between the plate and the cup and saucer. Tom rolled himself slowly to the edge of the plate. He could see as far down as the floor, through the pierced gaps in the plate decoration. It was a long way down, and it looked like a hard floor—he certainly wouldn't want to fall that far. If he could bridge the gap between the plate and the saucer then he could hide behind the cup and tell Rapunzel exactly what she needed to know. Under the cover of his cloak, and hidden by the slice of cake, he rummaged in his pocket. He found the useful ball of twine, perfectly shrunk under the spell. He attached the end of the twine tightly to an arrow head, lay along the plate, and held his bow sideways, from the prone position, and aimed across to the tea cup. If he could get the arrow through the handle of the cup he might just be able to pull himself over.

Snow White spoke suddenly, and very loudly, into the clock-ticking silence. Tom froze where he was.

'I know your name, I have just realized it. Why didn't I think of it before? We are saved, girls, for this is Sprightly the Sprite, is it not? I remember that there was a rotten little sprite called Sprightly who worked at the Bureau once; he vanished a while ago now.'

There was a roar of approval from all the princesses around the room.

'Huzzah for Snow White,' said Cinderella, 'she has saved us.'

The guard wolf sent up a howl; Ormestone, however, just laughed a great bone-chilling laugh.

'Ha ha ha, is that really the best you can do? Oh dear me no, this character here is certainly not "Sprightly the Sprite." What a ridiculous name, where on earth did you dredge that up from?' A collective sigh echoed around the room. The princesses would have to think again.

'One down and two to go,' said Ormestone. 'Think very carefully before you answer, very carefully indeed.'

The attention shifted back to the sprite. He was so relieved, so happy, that in his head he was dancing around on top of the pile of books; but really he was sitting with an impassive expression on his face, for he was now one answer closer to his great wish coming true, and he was consumed inside with relief, and happiness. His strange long feet in their black buckled boots suddenly kicked out on either side of him; his arms were folded, but the chair wobbled and he almost fell.

'Careful now,' said Ormestone balancing the chair, 'don't get too excited just yet.'

Tom took his chance and fired the arrow over the gap towards the tea cup. The arrow sped silently and shot straight through the handle space, and then Tom pulled at it, and sure enough the arrow turned and twisted and when he tugged the twine tight the arrow wedged itself up against the cup handle opening. Tom secured the other end of the twine tightly to a section of the cut out pierced lace pattern that ran around the edge of the plate. All was set, he waited for his chance.

Then Princess Zinnia stood up. She towered over the little sprite, who looked up at her and wobbled a little on his pile of books. She brought her arms up, closed her eyes, and pressed her hands to her temples. 'I'm getting something,' she said. 'I can feel an answer coming through from somewhere, something odd has happened.'

'Careful now,' said Sleeping Beauty.

'Are you sure?' said Snow White. 'Look what just happened to me, I was sure too.'

'Take care,' said Rapunzel.

'Go for it,' said Cinderella.

'I see something so clearly in my head, it must be connected to your name,' said Zinnia. 'I see white birds,' she concentrated, screwing up her face, 'white birds like angels, a cloud of white birds. Oh help, I don't know.' She sat down again. Then she stood up straight away, her eyes blazing. 'You are called Ludwig,' she said clearly and slowly, 'the swan king.'

The little sprite looked across at Ormestone, who simply raised his eyebrows. Then the little sprite coughed and shook his head. In his mind he jumped up and down on the pile of books, he danced with joy all over again. 'No, no, no, no, no, and again no,' he said and again he accidentally pushed his feet out and fell from the pile of books down on to the floor with a crash, spilling cups, and shattering plates and scattering slices of cake.

The confusion was total, and Tom took his chance. He jumped over to the length of twine, slipped his boots over the edge of the plate, grabbed hold of the twine, and swung himself down so that he hung by just his hands. He closed his eyes, gulped, opened his eyes again, took one quick look down at the chasm below his boots and began to move, hand over hand across the thick twine towards the safety of the tea cup and saucer.

Luckily the fall and crash of the sprite had caused chaos all around except for those princesses seated furthest from the mess. Rapunzel still sat calmly holding her cup and plate perfectly balanced, and Tom could see a look of wry amusement on her lovely face as she watched the little sprite struggle up from the muddle of china fragments and cake all over the floor. Tom tried his best to keep his eyes ahead on the saucer. His fear was that Ormestone would see him, or perhaps worse, that the guard wolf would.

Ormestone, however, was busy piling the books back on to the chair and helping the sprite up again, and the wolf was too busy eating all the spilled cake from the floor to notice anything at all. Halfway across the twine Tom looked down. He could see the cascade of Rapunzel's tattered wedding gown, a waterfall of silk muslin spilling on to the floor far below him and it seemed a very long way down. He carried on inching over, putting one hand over the other, and the twine swung a little as he moved across it.

He heard the wolf growl and Tom closed his eyes and froze just where he was. There was a scream from

Sleeping Beauty and another of the princesses said, 'Yuck.' After a second of waiting Tom opened his eyes. The attention of everyone seemed to be on the floor. Tom could see a sleek grey rat peeping from behind a chair, eyeing up a lump of the iced wedding sponge cake. The wolf stared at the rat and the rat inched back towards the wainscot. Tom thought it must be one of the rats driven out of the kitchen by the chef. Snow White stood up in a panic, Rapunzel stayed just where she was. Her cup and plate were still perfectly balanced. Tom gulped, braced himself and scrambled across the last inch or so of twine, and swung himself up into the saucer. He rolled behind the base of the cup, and waited. He could feel the warmth of the tea in the cup at his back.

He looked up and saw the huge face of the lovely Rapunzel. She was like a bright moon looking down at him. Tom raised his finger to his lips. Rapunzel saw him and then nodded slowly; she understood. Tom gestured that she should drink some tea, by raising his hand to his mouth. Rapunzel nodded again very slightly and then raised the teacup to her lips. Tom hung on to the little curl of china that finished the handle of the cup and was lifted with it. As soon as he was level with her shoulder he jumped down and landed among the folds of her dress. He clung on, and then climbed up and settled on her shoulder hidden behind the curtain of her hair. He cupped his hands and spoke as loudly as he could into her ear.

'I know his name,' Tom said. 'Jollity discovered it at the sprite's house in the woods, and Ormestone said it when I was hidden in the kitchen just before I was baked into the cake.'

He heard the gulp as Rapunzel swallowed a mouthful of tea, and then she whispered very quietly, 'You are sure?'

'Very sure,' said Tom.

The sprite was back on his feet, balanced again on top of the pile of books on top of the chair. He sat with his chest puffed out; he could barely contain himself. Ormestone had brushed him down and settled him and now there was only one attempted answer left, and after that the princesses would all be his for ever and ever after. His great wish would have come true. Here in the Land of Dark Stories, the land of unhappy endings, he would have his most wonderful wish fulfilled. Oh, how those poor pretty princesses would suffer; there was no going back now.

The wolf was sniffing the place where the rat had been and Ormestone called it to heel. Snow White sat down again.

'The rat has gone now,' said Ormestone. 'They are harmless enough, after all, just kitchen rats, nothing more. There are many much worse things in my kingdom, believe me; I should save your true fears for them when they finally appear,' and he laughed to himself.

There was silence in the room; most of the princesses seemed to be in a silent panic, apart from Rapunzel. She slowly put down her cup and saucer and stood up. All eyes turned to her. She put her hands down by her side and kept her head very still. She had noticed that Ormestone had put the Master's ceremonial sword down next to the cake; she had only to move her hand across just a little to be able to pick it up and use it. All that she needed now was a moment of confusion and distraction and she somehow felt that she was about to get just that and more.

'I think I know the answer to the question,' she said.

'Oh no,' said Snow White, 'careful now. Let's take our time, this is our last chance.'

'I know,' said Rapunzel, 'but it's worth a go.'

'A go?' said Cinderella. 'A go? We need something better than a go, we need to be sure.'

'Don't say anything yet,' said Zinnia, 'let's try and work this out; don't throw away our last chance.'

'It's going to go wrong again. Say nothing; wait, please wait. We are clutching at straws,' said Sleeping Beauty.

'The particular straw I'm clutching at is gold all through. All our straw is gold now,' said Rapunzel, 'sprite gold, perfect gold, all spun from straw. You don't really think that we did it all by ourselves, do you, your high and mighty majesty? We might be capable of many things but that trick was quite beyond us, I'm afraid.'

The sprite turned and looked directly at Rapunzel. His face had changed. Suddenly he looked frightened; fear and disappointment were being written on his face as she watched.

Ormestone turned his head to Rapunzel. 'Why, what in all the Land of Dark Stories can you mean?' he said.

'What I mean is that your little friend beside you on the chair, the one with the straggly little beard and all the magic tricks up his sleeve, did the gold spinning for us.'

The other princesses gasped together as one.

Ormestone turned his head to the little sprite. He was about to say something when Rapunzel interrupted.

'Don't you realize, he made all that gold because secretly he loves us, all of us. He wanted his own happy ending, to be married to all of us girls, isn't that right?'

The sprite turned his little head from one to the other, from Rapunzel to Ormestone. He looked up at his master and then he flicked his head again between the two of them, his eyes widening in panic. The wolf, sensing trouble now, and smelling once more the delicious scent of fear, got up from the floor where it had been lying and stood ready, tensed, with its tongue lolling from its mouth. A low mumbled growl started in its throat.

Rapunzel carried on, 'Oh, and one more thing, make sure you're kind to that poor sprite now; he can't help his feelings for us all. He must have had a rotten time growing up, what with a name like that.'

The other princesses looked at one another; here was a ray of hope. Rapunzel looked very calm, and very confident, could it be that she really knew the answer?

The sprite turned as white as a sheet of old Story Bureau letter paper. Panic gripped him and he reached down into his deep pocket and tried to pull out his little twisted stick of a wand; he might just be able to silence this girl, this lovely girl. He fumbled with the wand, as it was tangled in the folds of his breeches, but he was too late.

'Imagine, girls,' said Rapunzel, almost as an aside, 'going through life being called RUMPELSTILT-SKIN. You poor little thing, that is your name, isn't it?'

Ormestone stayed silent. Rumpelstiltskin froze where he stood, balanced on the pile of books, his face contorted with grief. Then he howled out loud, with a great cry of pain, and the wolf, sensing fun to come, joined in too and they set up an enormous noise between them.

When he had finished howling he said angrily, 'Who told you? Who told you? How in the Land of Dark Stories could you know? The devil himself must have told you.' The little sprite howled and his voice sounded like sobs.

He turned to look at Ormestone with a savage look on his face. Through all his tears and yells he still managed to finally drag his wand out of his pocket. Tom had watched everything from Rapunzel's shoulder. He saw at once that the little sprite, in his agony, might still be dangerous with the wand. He pulled his bow from his shoulder, loaded an arrow, and waited. Rumpelstiltskin, however, turned his wand towards Ormestone, his sallow little face red with fury.

'You must have told her my name,' he screamed miserably at Ormestone, and then levelled his stick wand like a weapon. 'You want me to suffer. You made the condition, you set the question, and then you answered it for them just to spite me, to make sure of my own unhappy ending,' the sprite cried, his arm wobbling. The wand waved about wildly in his hand, while dangerous looking little sparks of bad-tempered sprite magic flashed and flared from the end, and bounced off the walls and the teacups.

'I did not do any such thing, I can assure you,' said Ormestone smoothly. 'Now put that wand down. You can still have all these princesses for yourself; they aren't going anywhere, after all.'

Rapunzel took her chance. She reached across, and in one swift movement grabbed the Master's ceremonial sword from the table. She raised it up above her head with a flourish and the blade caught the light and flashed like a mirror; there was a sudden silence in the room.

Rumpelstiltskin moved his hand and the sparking wand across to face Rapunzel.

'Put the sword down,' he said, suddenly quiet and calm.

'No,' said Rapunzel.

'Chain them for ever,' said Ormestone.

Tom saw that his moment had come. He loosed his arrow and the sharp little tip struck Rumpelstiltskin and entered his wand hand. A flurry of sparks and stars flared from the end of the wand but were deflected from Rapunzel and instead struck the flat shiny silver of the sword blade and bounced back at Rumpelstiltskin. A set of iron manacles snapped instantly across his own arms. He dropped the wand and stood chained and wailing. Tom abseiled down Rapunzel's back using her long hair, and in the confusion no one saw him dash across the floor, hide under a chair, and load his bow again.

'You fool, see where your misguided ideas of romantic love will get you,' barked Ormestone. 'In chains. Now go and finish them,' he cried to the wolf, which stood ready and growling at his feet.

The wolf flattened its ears and stepped forward, its teeth suddenly bared, its tongue lolling out blood-red against the grey of its pelt. The princesses fell in line behind the figure of Rapunzel who held the sword out in front of her.

Rumpelstiltskin yelled out, 'No, no, not all my beauties,' and fell to his knees scrabbling to pick up the wand from the floor.

The wolf leapt up on to the table, scattering teacups, saucers, and plates. It lowered its head between its shoulders. It had seen what Rapunzel could do with a sword at the wedding and it was wary. Rapunzel moved back with the other princesses while Ormestone watched them with a look of amusement on his face.

'You will kill each and every one of them,' he said to the wolf. 'You will tear out their throats, do what you will, and when you have finished with them you will bring me all their pretty little heads in a row.' Ormestone chuckled, and then he went to the door. He spoke quietly, 'I half suspected that little Rumpelstiltskin was spinning the gold. He has disappointed me. For the sadly misguided love of you girls, well, obviously he would do anything. I shall leave him to enjoy the sight of your grim remains after the wolf has finished with you.' He went out quickly slamming the door behind him, leaving the wolf standing on the table, growling among the tea things.

'Coward!' screamed Rumpelstiltskin at the closed door. 'Coward, coward, coward,' he moaned to himself over and over as he shuffled across the floor on his knees. 'No, no, no,' he cried to himself as he pushed on towards the wand.

Then a roar erupted from the throat of the wolf, and Rapunzel stepped forward with the sword. 'It's all right, girls, it's all right,' she said as the wolf suddenly launched itself at her off the table with its dripping jaws wide.

Rapunzel slashed at the wolf with the long sword and the blade struck home. There was a curious noise, somewhere between a gargle and a soft wet explosion, and sparks and filaments of black and grey seemed to fly from the end of the sword where the wolf had once been. The air was full of streaks and grey smuts the colour of a wolf's pelt. A bent little figure landed back on the tea table all among the best china with a crash, and lay there for a moment. It was a grey goblin with a set of ferocious teeth. It sat up, looked at the line of princesses, snarled, and then dashed down from the table and scuttled out of the door as fast as it could. Little flecks and motes of grey fur still fell through the air.

The princesses all spoke at once in great excitement.

'How did you know his name? What was that thing? Come on, let's get out of here,' and so on.

Rapunzel saw out of the corner of her eye that Rumpelstiltskin had finally reached and made a grab for his wand and was now on his knees holding it out towards them in his chained arms, tears rolling down his face.

'I will keep you all with me for ever now,' he said quietly.

'I thought,' said Rapunzel, 'that if we answered the question, that if we knew your name, then we would be set free to marry the men of our choice?'

'You couldn't have known my name,' said Rumpelstiltskin.

'Oh, but I did though,' said Rapunzel.

'Yes, you did,' he added quietly, 'you did, but you must have cheated, he told you. You cannot leave me, any of you.' And he pointed the wand directly at the princesses.

247

Tom stepped out from the shadows under the chair. He held his bow out in front of him.

'Drop that wand,' Tom said as loudly as he could.

The sprite turned and saw Tom with the arrow pointing at his head, and then looked down at the little arrow still sticking out of his hand. 'So that was you,' he said, tugging at it.

'Yes, it was me,' said Tom. 'Tom Trueheart, of the adventuring Truehearts. I may be small, thanks to you, but I have been trained well with my bow, and I am a good shot as you can tell. I can load arrows very quickly too. Put down the wand, let the princesses go or I will fire.'

'And when Tom has finished I will cut off your head,' said Rapunzel, 'and deliver it to your master Ormestone.'

Rumpelstiltskin had not noticed, in his distraction and misery, that Rapunzel had moved quietly, like a whisper, on her slippered feet across the room and now stood over him, with the sword almost touching his skinny little neck.

'No, no,' sobbed the little sprite, 'don't hurt me.'

'First,' said Tom, 'what is Ormestone up to?'

'He likes gold, he collects gold.'

'It's more than that,' said Tom, pulling the string of his bow tighter.

'All right, all right, careful with that thing,' said Rumpelstiltskin. 'He has persuaded a whole army of the Dark Forces to help him. They will invade and destroy your own Land of Stories, but first he must pay them a certain amount of sprite gold for their trouble or they will not do his bidding.'

'How much gold?'

'I don't know; a certain weight, and it must be totally exact to the very last sprite gram.' Rumpelstiltskin bowed his head as if ashamed to be associated with anything so base, so mercenary, so business-like, so un-fairy-tale-like.

'You will restore young Tom to his rightful size now,' Rapunzel said.

'I must not,' Rumpelstiltskin said, 'or it will be the end for me.'

'It will be the end for you if you don't,' she said and pressed the sword blade tightly against his neck. 'I will do it too, you know I will.'

'Very well,' mumbled Rumpelstiltskin, and he

turned his still-chained arms towards the brave figure of little Tom, pointed the wand stick, and closed his eyes.

Chapter 28

Ormestone had left the wolf to do its worst, and now it was time to get back to the castle and await his army. He could do no more for the pathetic Rumpelstiltskin. He had been right to allow daily contact between the sprite and the princess brides; just look at the result. He had ingots and ingots of perfect sprite gold, and the Truehearts would really suffer now, and suffer for ever, when he finally dangled the princesses' pretty heads tied in a line on sprite ribbon in front of them all. He trudged on down the road, his black cloak flapping out behind him in the gloom.

A tall skinny figure was walking ahead of him, and as he drew closer, he saw that it was the scarecrow guard again, also marching off towards the castle, away from his post. He caught up with the scarecrow and it turned its broad pumpkin head, saw its master King Ormestone, remembered from before just what he had to do, and at once raised an arm in firm salute. As it did so, a big black crow suddenly flew off from the scarecrow's arms, up into the air above them, and the scarecrow watched it as it flew higher and higher away.

'Bad bird,' the scarecrow said quickly out of its mushy wide slit of a mouth, scattering pumpkin seeds as it spoke.

'Didn't seem very scared of you,' Ormestone said. 'Isn't that your job? Let's hope you're a better sentinel than you are a scarecrow. Was it one of my crows?'

'Bad bird,' the scarecrow said, spitting more pumpkin seeds.

'Never mind,' said Ormestone, 'I can see that we are going to get nowhere with this.' And he strode off ahead of the scarecrow, and hurried back to his looming Dark Castle.

Jollity flew as high as he could away from Ormestone

and the scarecrow. He turned and flew back down the road to the old palace, knowing that he might be needed there, and as soon as possible.

Chapter 29

Rumpelstiltskin, his head bowed, intoned some words, and then there was a spark and a flash of something that flew out from the end of the stick wand. Tom had readied himself, his eyes closed, and he waited for his transformation back to his normal size. The wand, however, was cunningly angled wrongly, and the spark missed Tom, and in an instant bounced off the large mottled mirror high on the wall behind him. It went instead straight back and struck Rumpelstiltskin who immediately vanished in a cloud of sparks, leaving his manacles and chains to fall slowly with a chink and clank to the floor. The sword blade was the next thing to hit the floor with a solid thunk, because Rumpelstiltskin's neck was no longer there to support it.

Rapunzel cried out, 'Curse you,' as she looked around. She poked the sword under the tables and chairs but the little sprite had gone, vanished.

Tom opened his eyes, his shoulders slumped.

'That's it, isn't it?' he said. 'He's gone and I shall stay this size for ever now.'

Rapunzel quickly picked Tom up and put him on the table. 'Don't worry, Tom, you brave boy, it will be sorted out, have no fear. In any case, Tom, however did you find us?'

'I was flying with Jollity, when I saw a flash of something white waving from one of the windows here. I thought that it might be a piece of one of your wedding dresses so we flew down to investigate.'

'I said that might work,' said Cinderella.

Then Tom told them everything that had happened to him, from his enchantment onwards, including that he had seen Jack.

'Do you know where your other brothers are now?' said Snow White.

'No,' said Tom miserably, bitterly disappointed not

to be back at his full size.

'They were taken to work a goblin gold mine,' said Rapunzel. 'It can't be far from here, they went on foot. Come on, we must all go now, it's surely our job to rescue them. Besides, that horrible Ormestone and his evil little sprite will be back soon enough with wolf reinforcements to finish us all. There is no time to lose; it's getting dark and we must at least try and rescue them. We shall all go at once. Will you join us, Tom?'

'My friend Jollity the crow was trapped by a scarecrow down in the garden. I got away, but I don't know what happened to him. I must find him first before anything else. As soon as I find my Jollity we will find you,' said Tom.

The princesses already had the Master's ceremonial sword, but they quickly searched the old palace for more weapons. They found an odd assortment of shields and rusty swords, pikes, and war hammers, enough to arm themselves, and they also found some old bits of uniform, moth-eaten, damp, but more useful for fighting than their tattered wedding dresses. They couldn't bring themselves to leave the wedding dresses behind so they bundled bits of armour and uniform over the top. They were quickly transformed into warrior princesses; Tom hardly recognized them. They looked a fearsome group as they all stood at the door ready to leave.

'Good luck,' Tom said. 'I will find you as soon as I can. I know Jollity, he will have escaped somehow, and will be looking for me.'

The rest of the palace was empty now and dark. The princesses took Tom down the steep stairs and out to the garden, and then they were soon gone, out on to the road, leaving Tom alone. He knew he wouldn't be alone for long. Ormestone or the sprite Rumpelstiltskin would surely soon be back, especially once the sprite wolf had reported what had happened to him. Tom went to the shrub near the kitchen door and retrieved his packstaff and went to the part of the garden where he had last seen Jollity.

The garden was in total darkness. The first thing Jollity would do surely was to come back to this place. A cold wind sighed in the trees all around him. There were the sounds of night creatures, too, all their clicking and buzzing noises, their moans and calls to each other. Tom sat on a bare patch of ground, away from the tall grass, which would have otherwise towered over him. He needed to be visible if Jollity was looking for him. Tom shivered. He was still miserable. He had come so close to regaining his normal size, it had been just a brief spark away, and then that horrible little sprite had denied him, had vanished and escaped. No matter, Tom would catch up with him at some point and force the spell to be reversed. He shook his head; how likely was that, after all, with Tom being the size of a thumb?

Perhaps the princesses could manage it? They had looked very imposing as warriors. Once they had found

Tom's brothers and rescued them who knew what might happen with them working as a team? How did he fit into it all now, what was there left for him to do at his size, useless and small? He wondered how Jollity would ever notice him sitting so tiny and helpless in the darkness. He drew his sword, and it crackled with reflected light and a brief flash shot up into the sky like a distress flare or a firework.

Jollity had been circling the palace using his crow night vision to look for Tom. He saw something flickering, moving in the garden, and he heard a keening noise. He flew down lower and saw none other than Ormestone's little sprite. He was tearing round the garden, striking out at the spiky bushes, kicking at things with his boots. The sprite fell to his knees. 'I love them all. Oh woe,' he cried and tore at his own beard and hit himself on the head. 'Oh, I've been a fool, a fool.'

The crow watched quietly from a hedge as the demented creature carried on crying and screaming out. Suddenly the creature stood up and began to pull and tear at one of his own short legs as if to pull it off. Then he stopped and ran off to the other side of the old palace where the stables were. A small balloon hovered on a tether there. There was a flash of glitter and light and the little creature hopped up into the basket. He cast off the rope and the balloon lifted into the air leaving behind his beloved princesses somewhere on the ground. He had an important mission to carry out now. 'If I can't marry the princesses then I will make sure those Trueheart brothers can't either.' He knew just what to do.

Jollity flew up and carried on looking for Tom; he had something really important to tell him now.

A few moments later a thin flash of light suddenly flared up from the garden below. Jollity flew lower and discovered he was back where the scarecrow sentinel had been standing. He could see a little line of reflected silver light down in the dark garden. He circled warily down, lower and lower. It was then that he saw that it was Tom sitting hunched over his birthday sword on a patch of dirt.

'Tom,' he called out, 'Tom it's me, Jollity.'

'Jollity,' said Tom sadly, 'are you all right? You escaped then; I knew you would.'

Jollity dropped to the ground. 'Oh yes,' he said. 'That scarecrow kept a tight hold of me for ever such a long time. He set off to take me to the castle, and then that awful Ormestone caught up with us and the daft, pumpkin-headed scarecrow went and saluted him, which meant of course he had to let go of me of a sudden, and I flew off back towards here as fast as I could. Then I saw little Rumpelstiltskin. I saw him just outside here. He was yelling and screaming all over the place, running up and down. "I love them all," he shouted. Then he started to try and tear himself into pieces, Tom, he tried to pull off his own leg. I've never seen the like before. Then he upped and disappeared in his balloon again just like he did in the woods, and I have a good idea where he's going too. Are you all right, Tom?'

'How could I be all right, Jollity. Look at me, at this pathetic size, I'm useless. What good am I to anyone being the size of a thumb; you'd be better off carrying on without me.'

'This isn't like you, Tom,' said Jollity. 'What happened to you in there, Tom, did you find any evidence of the princesses?'

Tom explained exactly what had happened since he had sneaked into the palace, including the cake, the questions, and all the rest leading up to Jollity finding him in the garden.

'Tom,' said Jollity, 'I think you just answered your own question. No one else could have done all that you just did. It was because you were so small that you were able to save them all, don't you see that?'

'I suppose so,' said Tom, brightening just a little. 'Let's go,' he added, 'we have to find and follow the princesses. They can't have got far—they went on ahead to rescue my brothers from the gold mine. It's up to us to stop Ormestone. His plans to invade the Land of Stories with the Army of Darkness are soon to be set in motion. He was going off to pay them in sprite gold.'

'That's better, that's more like the old Tom. Hop on, but let's be very careful shall we, that is one dangerous place, I reckon, Tom. Ready then?' said Jollity.

'Ready,' said Tom.

'Right, we've a fair distance to cover,' said the crow.

The bird lifted off from the garden, and Tom, in a moment of excitement as they rushed through the night air, pulled his birthday sword from his scabbard, raised it above his head, and called out, 'With a true heart,' at the top of his voice as they flew up into the darkening sky. As he spoke a few more little bright sparks and stars shot up from the tip of the sword into the air.

Part Three
Reunions and Reversals and Unhappy Endings for Some

Chapter 30

The little horse and cart drew to a halt. Ahead stood the goblin gold mine workings. A pit wheel could be seen and a group of low dark buildings all wreathed in cold mist. The horse had stopped for no real reason, she just knew she should stop at this place. Something inside her told her to follow Jack's trail to the goblin gold mine and then wait. Now that she had stopped the horse turned her head and looked for Jack, and there was more than a hint of sadness in the horse's eyes. There was no sign of her Jack or of anyone else. It was a bleak and desolate sight. The old mine working looked dark and closed and all broken down.

Why, that pit wheel's not even cabled up, the horse thought, and gave a mournful little whinny. All the way down that goblin gold mine to work, with all of your poor brothers. Don't see how anyone could work there, the horse thought. The cage couldn't even go up and down, without the wheel and the cables.

A single bell tolled suddenly loudly out of the fog; a lantern light was approaching slowly through the layers of mist.

Here comes someone. The horse lowered her head to the rough grass.

A tall shuffling man appeared. At first he was veiled by the rising fog, but he had very broad shoulders and he wore heavy-soled boots and carried the bright lantern. As he drew nearer the horse saw that it was a terrifying looking man with a stitched-up face, a silent lurching man.

The stitched-faced man ignored the horse and cart on the other side of the path. He hung the lantern on to a hook by the doorway to the mine workings, grunted to himself, then went inside the dark entrance. There was the roll and clatter of machinery, the turning of wheels, the pulling of ropes. The horse shifted in her shafts and shook her mane.

It was less than a minute later when a shambling

troll appeared out of the mine entrance. The troll was tall and stooped over and pushing a big barrow of ore and rock which was all piled up with shovels and picks on top. He was followed by another troll pushing a similar barrow which was piled even higher with darkly glittering ore. Behind them came the stitched-faced man, and a line of bent dusty figures all manacled together. There they stood, all lined up and exhausted looking, with their heads bowed, their Sunday-best wedding clothes all torn and tattered, their best white shirts flapping loose and covered in dark streaks of dirt and dust and at the end the last in the line was Jack with his head bowed. A little goblin stood beside them smiling a broad and chilling smile.

The stitched-faced man growled and held his lantern high. 'Urrrggggghhh,' he said and the goblin bowed low and spread his arms wide.

The Trueheart brothers stood quietly; Jack stood at the end of the line as if hypnotized.

'I don't like the look of this,' said Jackson, and straining against the manacle and chains he pointed up into the air.

The trolls and the goblin looked up too. A balloon

was slowly drifting down to the bleak earth. They could see a sprite peeping over the edge of the tall basket.

The goblin ran over and helped secure the anchor line. The sprite jumped out and came over to inspect the barrows of ore and the line of Trueheart brothers.

'Is that all the gold,' he said quietly, 'every seam exhausted, every last little chunk of ore?'

'Good gold all gone,' said one troll.

'No good gold left now, gold good, king's gold, all mined, king's gold all mined, all collected, all gone,' said the other.

'All gone, every last dot and speck, you are sure?'

'All gold gone,' they chorused in their low mournful voices.

'Good. I bring a message from our king. He is delighted with the trolls and their work but enough is enough and you may stop now. He has other uses for these Truehearts.'

The trolls grunted and lifted the barrow handles and began to push the heaps of gold ore away from the mine into the fog and darkness towards the smelting plant.

The sprite turned back to the goblin and the line of

Truehearts. He walked over to them, his dark cloak blowing about him, and his cold eyes fixed on the brothers one by one.

'What's happened to our brides?' said Jacquot with an expression of fury on his face.

'You have mined all the gold from the mine,' the sprite said, 'every last glint and trickle. You have worked well and hard, it is time that you were rewarded.' The sprite moved away, unsmiling.

'He asked you a question,' said Jacques. 'What have you done with our sweethearts?'

The sprite walked backwards from the line of Trueheart brothers, out of range of their anger.

'He goes away now,' said the goblin suddenly. 'He has taken back the *six* picks, and the *six* shovels, and the *six* lanterns, and you have mined the gold, *six* times over, now that there are *six* of you, at last, and is time to be going, going.'

The goblin turned and ran back to the mine. He scampered off on his long skinny feet, until he was swallowed up by the mine workings.

The brothers were left standing angrily in a line alone. The stitched-faced man walked backwards as well, leaving his lantern on the ground, and he was soon lost to view. His lantern shed its unearthly light across the brothers, and their long shadows spilled across the scrubby grass and harsh rocks. The horse watched everything carefully from the safety of the little cart, with a fast-beating heart. She kept very still, and made sure her head was lowered to the scrubby earth as she munched at the dry grass. She was worried about Jack, but luckily no one seemed to be taking any notice of her at all.

The brothers all called out together, in great confusion: 'You don't answer; have you nothing to say about the fate of our loved ones?'

Jack said, 'He told me he was going to a betrothal tea with all of them and he was to be the groom, and he doesn't deny it, I notice.'

The sprite shouted for them all to be quiet. He raised his arms for finally he was in charge. The Truehearts all stood with their manacled arms outstretched towards the sprite. He stood before them, his straggly hair and beard blowing in the bleak wind, his dark cloak swirling about him, his eyes glowing with cruel expectation. He smiled at them, at their eagerness to be free.

'I shall free you,' he said, 'all of you.'

'Yes, set us free,' said Jack, raising his arms. 'My brothers here, Jake, Jackson, Jackie, Jacquot, Jacques, and myself, need to be released from our manacles.'

'All shall be released, *all* of you, into freedom and also into beauty,' the sprite replied loudly, as he pushed his cloak back and stretched his arms out towards them.

'What is that supposed to mean?' said Jake. 'And to repeat, where are our beloved princesses?'

'Our king found another story start among all those documents and notes back at your sad Story Bureau. He charged me with the happy job of starting it all off, and now I shall finish my task: this will be the end of the beginning.'

'Whatever are you talking about?' said Jack, a terrible realization dawning.

The disappointed and betrayed lovesick little sprite from the tumbledown house in the woods closed his eyes and lowered his head. He kept his arm outstretched pointing the wand at the brothers. The wind increased, tipping over the mine lantern so that the light disappeared and they were all plunged into a sudden gloom. All was near darkness now except for the sprite's eyes, which he opened wide as he raised his head. His eyes glowed with a strange and brilliant light. Jack tried to step forward towards him, but found that he was fixed tight to the spot. The wind blew even harder, as the sprite flung his arms wide, and sang out into the rushing wind.

'I am cleansed, cleansed by water and by earth. I am charged, charged by fire and by air. The first star born to bring forth light, shall bring to this darkness white angels' wings.'

There was a blinding flash of white light, and a roll of thunderous noise. The horse let out a terrified whinny. She had realized exactly what might happen next, and decided it was time for her to act.

Chapter 31

TRANSFORMATIONS AND RESCUES
THE GOLD MINE
A SPLIT SECOND LATER

The horse reared and let out a huge whinnying sound and then galloped forward, pulling the cart as fast as she could. The sprite turned at the sudden noise, his hands still extended out towards the Trueheart brothers. The cart rushed over the scrappy grass and scrubland towards him, the horse with an expression of pure and determined fury on her normally placid, gentle face.

The sprite was startled, and he lost his concentration for just a split part of a second so that Jack's manacles and chains vanished and he alone was suddenly able to move. Jack ran at the sprite; he could see the oncoming cart. The sprite snapped his head back to the line of remaining manacled brothers and with startling speed bolts of white light shot out from his twig wand. The manacles on all the rest of the brothers' arms vanished too.

The cart suddenly soared over a ridge of grass, and cart and horse all seemed suspended high in the air for another frozen split second. Jack fell headlong across the grass and rolled over and over and landed on his back. The cart crashed to the ground inches from him and the ground shook as it struck.

Jack turned and looked over to where his brothers were. On the ground was a tangled heap of sprite-iron manacles and chains. Stepping out of the chains were five fine white swans, testing their wings. The swans called out sadly with mournful cries one to another. Jack sat up and stared in disbelief. His brothers had been turned into swans before his eyes.

Where was the little sprite? Jack stood up in a fury. He looked round to the place where the sprite had been standing, but he was already gone. He was up and running very fast across the dead grass back to the balloon. Jack saw his bow on the floor of the cart, grabbed it, raised it, fitted an arrow against the twine, pulled it taut and aimed it at the sprite's retreating back. However, he couldn't fire the arrow as his five swan brothers were suddenly in the air between him and the retreating sprite. He just had to watch as the sprite ran away and jumped up into the balloon basket and sailed quickly up into the air.

The balloon was too high, perhaps, for Jack's good aim to reach but it was still worth a try. He fired his crow-flight arrow towards the balloon. It was impossible to say if it had struck or not, and he watched the balloon sail away towards the castle. He walked over to the cart and patted the horse affectionately. 'You saved me, I reckon,' he said, while the five swans, his brave brothers, flew just overhead together round and round above him calling out plaintively into the dark.

Chapter 32

Towards the Dark Castle Again
Later

The princesses were soon on the road. Buoyed up by their sudden freedom, they ran like school-girls. After a while though, tired of running, they slowed to a walking pace. They were not long on the dark road when they came across the strange figure of the walking scarecrow lumbering along in front of them.

'What a strange thing,' said Cinderella.

'Horrible,' said Sleeping Beauty.

'Creepy,' said Snow White.

'It might just know the way to the gold mines though,' said Zinnia.

'Good thinking,' said Rapunzel.

They quickly formed a circle around the staggering skinny object. It stopped and doffed its hat to them.

'Good evening, ladies,' it said with its wide mushy pumpkin grin, seeds dribbling from its slash of a mouth.

'We are sent by the king to the gold mines,' said Rapunzel, her hand firm on the pommel of the sword. 'Perhaps you could tell us where they are?'

The scarecrow saluted at the use of the word 'king', and then turned its round head and raised the other stick-thin arm in its ragged sleeve and pointed its brittle gloved hand across the plain. 'Over there,' it said spraying seeds again.

'Thank you,' said Rapunzel, and they all moved away from him and turned in the direction he had pointed. But the scarecrow lunged forward and held on to Cinderella's arm.

'Let go,' she shouted.

Rapunzel drew her sword and spoke to the baggy stick creature. 'Please let my friend go,' she said quietly.

Cinderella could feel the twig fingers inside the glove tightening on her arm. 'Ow,' she said.

'You are the king's ladies,' said the scarecrow mushily. 'The king's ladies, all belong to the king,' it said again, spitting out more seeds at them, its grip still firm on Cinderella's arm.

'Trick or treat, Mr Pumpkin-head Scarecrow?' said Rapunzel.

'Treat,' said the scarecrow hopefully through its slash of a grin.

'Wrong answer,' said Rapunzel. 'It's trick, I'm afraid,' and with one blow of the ceremonial sword she separated the grinning pumpkin head from the twigs and ragged clothes of the scarecrow's body. The pumpkin fell to the ground and lay at their feet still grinning up at them.

'We belong to ourselves, not your king.'

The scarecrow's body shivered a little where it stood and then collapsed on itself, into a tattered bundle of old rags and sticks and twigs.

'Yuck,' said Sleeping Beauty.

'Ugh,' said Zinnia.

'Good riddance,' said Cinderella.

'Very creepy,' said Snow White.

'Best use for a scarecrow,' said Jollity, suddenly flying down among the girls with Tom on his back.

'Is that Tom?' said Cinderella. 'Well done. You obviously found your friend the crow then?'

'Oh yes,' said Tom. 'Everybody, this is my good friend and adventuring companion Jollity the crow.'

'Welcome, Jollity,' the girls chorused.

'This way,' said Rapunzel, sheathing the sword. 'We are on track to go and rescue your brothers, Tom.'

The princesses, Jollity, and Tom set off in the direction that the scarecrow had pointed out.

They had not travelled far across the cold and scrubby plain before they heard the rattling squeak of a set of cartwheels and the mournful honking of swans coming towards them muffled by the mist. It was hard to make anything out in the gloom and there was certainly nowhere to hide. Rapunzel drew the sword and the princesses stood their ground in a line across the path and waited for whatever was in the cart to emerge from the mist.

Jack spoke kindly to the horse, reassuring her as he peered into the murky plain ahead of them.

'Come on then, old thing,' he said, 'we'll soon bed down for the night.' He had grown very fond of the horse. It had pulled the cart all on its own and followed him, for some reason, faithfully all the way to the gold mines and with almost no sign of tiredness or complaint. The horse slowed suddenly and then stopped altogether. Something was in front of them right across the road. 'Whoa,' said Jack. He let go of the reins, slipped his bow from his shoulder, and stepped down from the cart.

Jack walked forward, and called out, 'I've got you covered, there's no escape.'

A woman's voice answered him, 'We have you covered as well, and there are five of us here and we are all armed.'

'Oh really,' said Jack. 'Well, there are lots of me as well; we're just now advancing on all fronts.' He stepped nearer to the voice, and saw a line of shadowy armed figures across the road in front of him. It was too late, they had seen him, and suddenly he was Simple Jack all over again.

'Jack?' said a voice from in front of him.

'Jack Trueheart?' said another.

'It is him,' said a third.

'Oh my,' said a fourth.

'At last,' said a fifth.

Jack was engulfed on all sides by a sudden deluge of hugs and kisses. It was the princess brides, all five of them, and they looked armed and very dangerous.

'So all of you escaped,' he said. 'And Tom and Jollity too. Here you all are. Now we are really getting somewhere,' he added nervously.

The princesses clustered round Jack.

'We were on our way to the goblin gold mine to rescue you and your brothers, Jack,' Zinnia said.

It was then that more mournful honking noises came from the sky just above them and the five white swans gracefully landed nearby, stretching their wings.

'Now about my brothers,' said Jack. 'I am afraid you must be prepared for a shock. I have some awful news to tell you about them.'

After the tearful reunion, when each girl had tried to identify her particular swan boy, and all had hugged as best they could, they vowed to travel on together to the castle. The five swans flew close overhead glowing white in the darkness, letting out an occasional 'honk'

to let everyone know that they were still there. The horse kept up her steady pace, while Jack urged her on in his best kindly voice. Tom and the crow flew among the swans above the cart. The princesses took turns two at a time to ride in the cart.

Jack drove on towards the looming tower of the castle but inside he was feeling a little dazed and confused. He had only just been saved from being transformed into a swan by the woodcutter's horse making a diversion at just the right moment. The more he thought about that moment the more deliberate it seemed; it was as if the horse wanted to save him especially.

The horse kept a good eye open on the road, turning her narrow head and looking fondly up at Jack every now and then. Occasionally one of the swans would fly down and land on the cart and honk or croon quietly to Jack or one of the princesses. Jack would talk back to them.

'We'll find a way to reverse the spell, don't you worry. Jack's here now, and Tom and Jollity, and your lovely brides too, just look at them. All will be well in the end. Ormestone will be the only one to suffer a really unhappy ending, I promise you that,' said Jack.

These were brave words, and Jack and the horse, and all the princesses and the five swan brothers and Tom and his crow friend could only hope that those brave words really would come true.

Just a little way down the road, some way behind the cart, strode the angry woodcutter and her husband. They had walked non-stop all day towards the Dark Castle to report the fugitives and their many crimes. The man carried a rolled-up copy of the king's proclamation in his hand, which he was only too willing to show to whoever they might meet. From time to time the woodcutter thought about the tiny little boy, who was her wish fulfilment, and how ungrateful he had been for being saved by them.

Now, however, it was getting dark and the poor superstitious couple were far from home. As the light failed, so their steps began to slow down, and the slightest rustle in the bushes, or the crack of a twig, caused them to panic, and the woodcutter to heft her axe and think of hungry wolves. Then there came an enormous crashing sound from nearby as if something large had fallen straight out of the sky and landed among the trees and bushes just in front of them. There followed a whole bout of rustling noises so close to them that they stopped walking altogether. Something was there in the bushes in front of them, and it seemed to be getting nearer. It was grumbling and muttering curses, whatever it was. The little man held on to his wife, hid behind her in fact, but then she was much taller than he was.

'Careful now, dear, remember I'm here to protect you,' he said, holding out the rolled paper proclamation from behind her back and waving it threateningly in the air.

'How could I forget,' she said.

They stood together waiting in the gloom, afraid to either go forwards or back, when suddenly a cross and dishevelled little man stepped out on to the road. He seemed out of breath, and he held a little stick in his hand. 'Good evening,' he said.

'Good evening,' said the woodcutter, shouldering her axe and giving a hint of a curtsy. She sensed that here was someone odd looking, magical even, a sprite of some kind, they had better be careful.

'I am on my way to the Dark Castle and I trust that this is the right road,' the little man said.

'We are travelling there ourselves, sir,' said the woodcutter.

'Oh yes,' said her husband, 'we are on our way to report some fugitives. They stole our best cart and our poor horse; a couple of "wish fulfillers", that the king seeks, and even offers a fine reward for.'

'Was there a half-witted youth?' said the sprite, his eyes narrowing.

'Exactly so,' said the woodcutter, 'and of course that tiny little boy we found,' she added.

'Yes, the tiny little boy,' said the sprite, 'and that oaf. I wish them so much harm. Oh, and by the way, they will have worn out your sad horse by now too.' And the sprite sniffed and wrinkled up his nose as if in disgust at the thought.

'Perhaps you would care to join us on the last part of our walk to the castle. It won't be far now and we could keep you company, if you would like,' said the woodcutter's husband.

'Oh yes, indeed,' said the woodcutter.

'You look like a strong woman,' said the sprite.

'Oh yes indeed I am,' said the woodcutter.

'She is, very strong and hard working, too, aren't

you, my dear,' said her husband.

'Yes I am, dear, thank you.'

'In that case,' said the sprite, 'I wonder if you would carry me for a while on your ample back.'

'Oh,' said the woodcutter, taken aback, 'well, I don't know . . . '

'I'm so tired and worn out, with fulfilling all my duties to our king. If you were to do me that favour I'll grant you one in return. I have certain powers; for instance, I can grant you a special wish,' said the sprite.

'Now, now,' said the woodcutter's husband, 'wish fulfilment is banned by our king, but on this occasion he offers such a thing, a wish fulfilment, as a special reward for finding these fugitives.'

'The king is a very good friend of mine,' said the sprite with a sour expression on his face. 'I was working for him today. Indeed, I was carrying out very important wishes of his own.'

The woodcutter looked at her husband, and the husband shrugged his shoulders.

'Typical,' he whispered, 'the king is allowed any number of wishes, and we're not.' And he shook his head.

'Yes, my dear, it was always like that. But this kind gentleman has offered us our own wish as payment, and a bird in the hand is worth the two in the bush of a possible reward. Who's to say we'll ever find those fugitives again? I reckon this time we'll get it right; no more sausages or horses, if you take my drift. Come on then, sir.' The woodcutter bent over and gestured to her strong back. The sprite clambered on to the woodcutter, and settled himself.

'If we do find the fugitives then we shall bring them to justice too, and you can claim the king's wish as well as mine,' said the sprite. And so it was that they all three set off hurrying up the road towards the Dark Castle.

289

Chapter 33

THE ARMY OF DARKNESS
11 P.M.

Jack heard something behind them: a steady muffled rhythm. He listened, and then pulled the horse to a halt. 'Come on,' he called, 'into the bushes, everyone, and quick.'

He and the princesses helped to pull the horse and wagon off the road in among the dark shrubs and the tangle of bushes and briars. The swan brothers and Tom and Jollity flew silently above them in a circle.

'Ssh,' said Jack, his beefy finger up against his mouth. 'Soldiers coming, by the sound of it.' His eyes widened and he crouched down low among the twisted prickly branches. The princesses lined up behind him. Jack held the horse's head close and tenderly against his chest.

'If we stay nice and quiet here and just let them go by we should be all right,' he whispered to everyone and then repeated it even more quietly in the horse's ear. The horse flicked her mane and kept her head close to Jack.

The sound of the marching drums grew louder. Jack kept himself well back from the road, but he had a good view through a gap in the hedge. The first line of troops appeared. Jack watched them ride past, a host of cavalry men in black cloaks. One of the soldiers turned and looked in Jack's direction from his horse, and a red light seemed to pierce the dark from where the soldier's eyes were. What Jack saw made him shiver. He pulled his head back from the hole in the bush. It was time to move, and as far away as possible.

'Princesses,' he whispered, 'I think we should move further into the trees and find some sort of secure shelter for ourselves. I'll tell you why in a moment.'

So Jack led the horse and cart as quietly as he could away from the drumbeats and the marching boots through the undergrowth and into a dense little wood.

After what seemed a long time they came to a rough clearing with a round dark lake, and there they stopped. The pale shapes of the five swan brothers were soon floating on the dark surface. The princesses went over and sat on some logs by the water near Jack. Jollity and Tom flew down and settled beside them too. Jack seemed shocked; he was trembling.

'We really need to find somewhere proper to hide,' said Jack. 'I have to warn you, princesses, Tom, Jollity, old friends, that what I just saw made my hair stand on end. I have just seen the Army of Darkness and they were,' he paused and looked around and then he whispered, '*skeletons*, every last one of them, even the horses.'

'A terrible army indeed,' said Zinnia.

'Skeletons?' said Tom.

'Skeletons?' repeated the other princesses.

'Need a safe place to hide,' said Jack.

The horse gave a worried little whinny.

Tom walked forward along the log and called out for everyone to listen.

'We don't need a hiding place,' he said, 'we know what we have to do. We can't sit back and hope for the best; we must go forward now and finish what we've started. At the moment we are all together, but I think there are too many of us and that we will stand a better chance in smaller groups. I would suggest that Jollity and I fly on to the Dark Castle and you all follow across the fields and woods away from the army. We'll meet somehow in that awful place.' He gestured with his sword towards the Dark Castle, and a little flash of silver ran down the blade.

'Well done, Tom,' said Jollity.

'You are quite right, Tom,' said Jack. 'We must do this the Trueheart way, the adventurer's way. I shall take the cart and the swans with me as if for market, and the princesses shall make their way through the woods.'

'A good plan,' said Rapunzel, standing and raising her sword like Tom. All the princesses stood then and raised their weapons. 'With a true heart,' they chanted, and the swans set up a chorus of proud honks.

Tom and the crow were the first to near the castle which towered over the horizon. The tall pinnacles vanished into the lowering dark clouds that seemed to whirl all around the top. The crow alone knew, of course, that the rolling dark cloud was made up of thousands of vicious sentinel crows and bats. Tom clung on to the feathers of his friend, glad to be flying with him again, even if he had just come so very close to being restored to his full size. He was sure that there would be another chance.

Then below them on the road, Tom suddenly heard the sound of the army marching: the deep bass thump of marching drums. Tom looked down through the mist and gloom. It was hard to make them all out clearly but there seemed to be hundreds of them, thousands even, cavalry, wagons, and infantry. There was something very strange about them as well, a kind of ghostly glow; the faces from such a height and distance looked very pale, almost chalk white.

'Do you see them down there, Tom?' said the crow.

'Yes,' said Tom, 'that's them. Looks like Jack was right.'

'The forces of darkness,' said Jollity. 'Ormestone's invasion army. I think we should swoop down for a closer look,' said the crow, dipping his wings towards the ground.

They drifted down lower, the crow flapping his wings

as quietly as he could, making almost no noise at all swooping down in wide circles towards the road. When they were close enough to see the troops clearly, Tom clapped his hand over his mouth to stop himself from crying out. The horses of the cavalry, the soldiers on their backs, the marching troops, with the muffled marching drums, the lines of buglers, were all indeed skeletons. A whole army of bones, stretched all along the road towards the castle, and as far back as the eye could see.

Jollity flew straight above their skull heads for a while. It was just then that they were spotted by a skeleton bugler. It looked up at the same moment that Tom looked into its white face and Tom glimpsed the black eye sockets, and deep inside a pair of bright red eyes like torches or lanterns looking back up at him. The mouth of the creature opened and let out a dry sort of squawk, then the gleaming bugle was raised to its mouth and a shrill blast of alarm sang out into the darkness.

'Time to go, Jollity,' said Tom.

'I'm ahead of you there, Tom,' said Jollity, beating his wings fast and pointing himself straight up into the dark sky. The bugle call rang out behind them, over and over, like an alarm signal, which, of course, is just what it was.

'Did you see them?' Tom gasped, his heart beating faster. 'There were so many of them; they were horrible, horrible.'

'What a terrible sight, Tom,' Jollity replied, 'and I don't like that trumpet thing either, they're warning someone or something.'

The castle loomed even bigger now, blotting out what little drab foggy light there was. It was so tall that Tom had to crane his neck to look up at the top of it and that was from the air. The rolling black cloud that hovered over the tower looked very strange now that they were closer to it. The bugle call from below seemed to have set something moving. Part of the cloud detached itself, and seemed to be flying towards them. It was as if the cloud were unravelling itself in a dark spiral of flapping leathery black shapes . . .

. . . BATS.

Tom gasped when he realized what was heading towards them very fast; not just a murder of crows, but a whole army of big bats too, on the wing. Tom gripped on tightly to Jollity's neck. There was no need to say anything. The huge malicious cloud of black wings, claws, and beaks all mixed up together, flew straight at them. Below them was the skeleton army, above them now the great cloud of bats and crows, and ahead stood the Dark Castle itself, the evil centre of the Land of Dark Stories. They had no choice but to go straight on to the castle and find some semblance of shelter and safety.

As if by a prearranged signal, the cloud of birds and bats dived down towards them in one shrieking group. Tom pulled his birthday sword from the scabbard, and this time there were even more sparks and flickers of bright light from the blade than there had been before. It was as if the sword blade had been woken up by something. That thing his mother had meant to tell him about the sword? He was soon distracted from any more thoughts like that by the shrieking dark forces that were about to tear into them. He held Jollity tightly with his knees and gripped his sword with both hands.

The first wave of bats and birds suddenly surrounded them like a whirlpool and Tom slashed out with his little sword. The sword did more than spark. It flashed like lightning, great bolts of white light soaring up from the tiny strip of metal, cutting great holes in the clouds of bats and crows. The blaze of crackling light cut a path through the dark wings. Clouds of smoke, soft explosions, glitter, and fragments and feathers fluttered in the sky as hundreds of spells were broken all around them and the dark masses, whole groups of bats and crows, became just single tumbling sprites which fell past them, opening their special black falling cloths as they floated down to the army below. Tom and the crow burst through the masses of bats and birds until they were at the edge of the Dark Castle itself.

Tom sheathed the sword and they were once more cloaked in darkness. Jollity flew down and landed on a window ledge high on the central tower. Tom was shaking. 'I could feel the power in my sword, it felt alive in my hand,' he said. 'I don't understand; the light, the sparks, look how it cut through them all, and it's only small.' Tom patted the sword handle at his side.

'I think I understand, Tom,' said Jollity catching his breath. 'I know things. I hear things. I think you were meant to be told this much later on, but the way things look as if they are going now, there may not be a much later, Tom.'

'Don't say that, we'll find a way, Jollity.'

'I hope you're right, Tom, but look at all those awful creatures, that army and this terrible place.'

'This is not like you at all, Jollity,' said Tom.

'I know. I'm sorry, Tom, but seeing that whole dark army of skeletons has shaken me, worried me, properly worried me. Listen, I can hear their terrible drums now.'

There came the distant, muffled, marching beat like thunder approaching the castle. Tom could just hear it over the squawking birds and the bats which still circled the turret.

'Your father made your sword, Tom,' said Jollity. 'He forged it in the Land of Myths and Legends using special sprite metal. I think the spell you are under has gradually woken its power, even though it has been reduced in size.'

Tom pulled the sword out from the scabbard.

'No, Tom,' said Jollity, but his warning was too late, the sword immediately shone out like a bright lantern.

The circling birds and bats swooped out of the sky in a rush down towards the bright light. Tom dropped the sword onto the ledge and it all went dark again but the squealing bats were soon on to them. Tom felt the cold wind from their leathery wings, and he pushed

himself back in the darkness, but he lost his footing and fell through the arrow slit window and down into the turret itself.

Tom found himself falling through the darkness inside the tower. He had left his sword on the ledge, and was tumbling now through dark space; he had no idea where he was falling to or what he might find there when he finally hit the ground.

Chapter 34

INSIDE THE DARK CASTLE
THAT NIGHT

Julius Ormestone, once a story deviser, now the self-styled king of the Land of Dark Stories, sat in his cobwebbed throne room. He could hear the thumps of the muffled marching drums. It was the approaching Army of Darkness. He had been disturbed earlier by the arrival of an angry goblin. The goblin was normally transformed as a guard wolf at the old palace. It was in front of him now kneeling on the steps that led up to the dark throne.

'You say that one of those princesses plunged the sword into you?'

'Yes . . . *cough* . . . Master,' said the goblin, little bits of coughed-up grey fur fluttering from his mouth every time he spoke. 'She may have attacked your personal sprite too . . . *cough*.'

'And when the sword touched you your spell was broken?'

'Yes.'

'Well, well, that's the second time, interesting. So my poor familiar, my "Rumply stilty" boy may well be no more. Well, it seems the fool lost all sense and actually fell in love; he deserved all he got, especially at their hands. He should have learned to just do my bidding and all would have been well, a lesson you should all learn. Very well then, you are my special assistant now; stay close, I may have need of you. Come, follow me, the army approaches.'

Chapter 35

A Strange Meeting
The Dark Castle

Jollity picked up Tom's little sword in his beak and, forced by the pressure of the whirling birds and bats flapping all around him, he allowed himself to fall backwards through the window. He soon recovered his balance, and flew steadily downwards inside the tower, turning slowly around the dank curves of the thick wall. It was even colder inside the castle than outside, and he hoped that Tom had landed safely on one of the steps of the twisting staircase, because it was a very, very, tall tower and it was a long way to fall. Jollity flew on down looking for any sign of him.

Tom Trueheart was flat on his back lying on a step halfway down the tower. He had gone into free fall, and only his billowing winter cloak had broken his descent. He now lay awkwardly on the cold dark stone. Tom sat up and shivered. He could hear the shrieking birds and bats echoing some way above him, and he also thought that he caught the faint sound of his friend Jollity the crow calling out for him, but from some way further down, a long way below in the pitch darkness. There was nothing for it now, he would have to climb very carefully all the way down the steps.

He rolled himself forward to the edge of the step and when he looked over he saw that the stairs clung to the curve of the wall. The steps snaked away below him in a dizzying spiral which went down and down as far as he could see. At one point he thought that he could still just hear the sound of Jollity calling out to him, but his voice seemed more vague and distant now, almost vanished in the eerie silence below.

Each step had a deep rise, especially deep if you were the size of a thumb. He had to work out a safe way of getting himself down each step as if it were a sheer stone cliff face. He swung his legs over the edge gripping tightly to the step. He let his feet dangle out into space and then felt with the toes of his boots for any possible holds and supports such as cracks or faults in the stone. These stairs were very difficult to judge. The sheer drop on the side was deep, and the tower itself seemed to go on down for ever. The steps were damp and slippery, and as he climbed down each stair, the thought of what Jollity had just told him filled his mind. His precious birthday sword was more precious than he had imagined. He had thought it a good plain workmanlike sword until he had used it just now, and had felt that sudden surge of power guiding his hands. His own birthday sword, and forged, it turned out now, by his father, and not only that, forged in the Land of Myths and Legends too. Perhaps that was what his mother meant to tell him on the wedding morning? Now he had lost it for ever, he felt awful.

He kept on climbing down until he reached one of the many narrow buttress bridges which crossed from the staircase to the corridors on the other side of the tower. He decided to explore the nearest of the corridors. He disturbed a large cobweb which stretched between the corner of the step and a rusty iron support chain. As Tom brushed off the sticky filaments and turned to go into the corridor, something scampered down the long strand of web, something bloated but hungry that had waited a very long time for something fresh to eat.

The corridor led into the main part of the castle. It was lit with torches which had a sputtering cold blue flame. Tom could see rows of doors ahead of him on either side of the corridor. Two sprite guards stood outside one of the doors. Tom crossed the bridge carefully. He half walked and half ran along the corridor and looked up at the guards outside the door. They were both asleep, slumped against the wall on either side. The door was made of black wood and there was a skull and crossbones painted on it, in the strange glowing luminous white paint that seemed to be everywhere and on everything in the Land of Dark Stories. Below that was painted just the one word, again in big glow-in-the-dark letters:

LIBRARY

Tom thought that there were most likely spell books

and old works of magic locked away in such a library in this place. If he could find the right book then there was a good chance that he might be able to reverse the spell on himself. It was worth trying. Why else would such a room be guarded? He looked for a way in. The simplest thing seemed to be to just quietly roll under the gap at the bottom of the door, and so he did, ploughing as he did through heaps of dust and old cobwebs.

Something followed him in, a moment or two later, something fat, and pale, and round, something that only just managed to get its bloated body through the same gap.

Tom emerged into the dimly lit library. He was covered in dust and strands of cobweb. He coughed and spluttered for a while and then he brushed off as much of the dust and filaments of cobweb as he could, and then looked around. Every wall was lined with shelves of books. They stretched up as far as he could see, right up to the vaulted ceiling. There was a big table in the middle of the room. Tom set off warily across the floor. Then he became aware of a presence in the room. It was as if someone had crept in behind him very, very quietly. He felt a tingle on his neck, and all the hairs on his nape stood on end. Old Cicero Brownfield would have said that 'someone had walked over his grave'. It was just as if he were being watched closely by someone or something only just behind him, hidden somewhere in the deep shadows. He kept very still. He did not dare to look round even though he felt that he was just imagining it.

Then he heard a scratching noise, something sharp and spiky. Something, somewhere above him, was moving fast on pointed claws. It sounded as if it was moving across a dry and brittle surface. He heard a sigh; so there was someone in the room, after all. Tom thought of the kitchen rats at the palace that had been banished to the princesses' rooms. There must be many more such rats in a castle like this. The noise came again, and it was definitely a human sigh of boredom.

'Urgh, dear me,' it said.

And then there was a creaking sound, like someone stretching in an old chair. It would be no use Tom calling out to them, his voice would not carry. In any case they were not likely to be friendly in this place. He walked a little further forward, and looked beyond the edge of the thick carved table leg. He could see an enormous foot in an enormous shoe and beside it another. They were old buckled boots. Tom could clearly see that the silver buckles were tarnished, and that whoever was wearing the boots had let them go into holes, and they were literally down at heel.

So, a poor person by the look of things, perhaps a lowly scribe, Tom thought, and he walked slowly over to the table leg. He was looking for footholds in all the twists and carving on the table leg when he felt something soft and light touch his neck. He put his hand up to touch it and felt some sticky strands of something. A piece of cobweb perhaps, that he had failed to brush away? While his hand was still there, another fine sticky filament fell on him; he actually felt it land on his skin. He turned round.

Tom found himself looking into the wet, sticky, working jaws and the dark, fierce eyes of a pale, bloated spider. The spider towered over him. Tom froze in terror. He could hear the scratching sound again, coming from somewhere above him on the table, but the table was out of reach now. The spider moved forward. Tom could see the fine hairs on its legs, and it seemed to have so many of them. It moved with quick little jerky movements, movements that Tom remembered so well from his garden at home when he had teased spiders, when he had pushed at or broken their webs with his toy sword or a stick, and had watched them run in panic.

The spider's jaws were still moving. It seemed suddenly to spray or spit at him, and a great glob of something sticky landed on his legs. Tom turned and moved away, tried to run, but the spider was fast and it scuttled after him. He felt one of its legs touch him, and Tom let out a terrified yelp. It was then that he remembered what Jack had said about the spiders' poison sac, and how they could give you a nasty bite if they wanted. He wondered how that poison would feel now, now that he was so very small.

Tom tripped on all the new filaments that seemed to be fast covering him. He rolled over, only to look up into the moving jaws of the spider. The spider's legs were all around him. He was trapped, pinned down. He automatically reached for his sword, only to remember that he had lost it. He had no weapon to use and he found that he could hardly move his arms; the sticky web filaments were falling so fast around him that it seemed they would soon cocoon him completely. Tom couldn't allow this to happen. He had to act and act quickly.

He wrenched both his arms free and rolled vigorously from side to side loosening the filaments. He felt a slight surge of power in his sword arm and moved very fast. He pulled himself upright so that he was directly under the pale belly of the spider whose body hung over him like a big wet bag. He closed his eyes and pushed himself free of the legs, and turned as the spider came at him. He looked into its fierce eyes, and it spat at him again. Now Tom found he was able to move so fast that he was easily able to dodge the sticky spit as it flew through the air at him, in fact, he parried it with his hand and flicked it harmlessly aside. He made for the table, trailing bits of filament after him as he ran. The spider scuttled after him.

Tom leapt for the table leg. He clung on and began to climb among the carvings on the table. The hungry spider came after him. Tom found that he was a quick climber now, quicker than he could ever remember being before. He seemed to have a sixth sense about footholds and distance. He was easily outrunning the spider, and the spider was fast. Tom hauled himself on to the top of the table and quickly surveyed the terrain all around him. There were books in dusty heaps, a few bowls, a pestle and mortar, and bulbous glass flasks and retorts.

And there was a man.

A man wearing gold-rimmed glasses sat at the far end of the table in a warm pool of light cast from a single candle. He had a quill pen poised in his hand. Tom had no choice, he had to trust his instinct, and he ran across the table top. The spider ran close behind him, still spitting filaments of sticky web. Several books stood open among all the equipment. They had black pages, and the printed writing was all done in that same glowing white ink. Tom jumped up and ran across the nearest of them, and then he fell right down into the channel at the centre of the book, and then he ran right up the hill of the opposite page. He reached the top edge of the thick book and turned; the spider was making fast progress behind him.

He jumped down from the book, landed awkwardly and only just picked himself up in time. The spider was soon on to him again and running fast on its awful hairy legs. He had little choice but to run straight towards the man who was writing so carefully at the end of the table. There was nowhere else to go. He ran as fast as he could, his legs pumping, kicking up book dust as he went. He would surely be seen at any moment by Ormestone's henchman, and that would be that. But, he thought, it would be better than being attacked by a giant spider in a filthy sticky cocoon.

He turned, just to see where the spider had got to. There was no doubt that it would soon catch him. Tom had no choice but to run straight on to the very page that the scribe was working on. Tom seemed in the last few seconds to have slowed down, as if he had used up a whole store of his inner energy very quickly. He had reached the middle of the page when he heard a friendly booming voice.

'Hello, what's all this? Goodness me, I really have gone mad now.'

Tom was aware of a shadow passing overhead and a flash of something. Then there was an enormous thump on the paper he was standing on. It was like an earth tremor, and it knocked Tom off his feet. He fell and lay on his back for a second, his eyes closed, fearing the worst. He heard the voice again.

'Now I know I'm mad,' the voice said. 'Ah me. Well, it had to happen sooner or later.'

Tom sat up and looked behind him expecting to see the spider's jaws ready for the kill. He did indeed see the spider, but it was walking round and round, pacing across a loose piece of black paper, firmly secure underneath an upturned wine glass. The paper and the glass were lifted away and Tom heard the creak of a window being opened, and then he heard the voice say, 'Off you go, take care now,' then the man turned back to the table.

'Don't worry, little figment of my imagination,' said the voice to Tom, 'she can't harm you now, and I haven't harmed her either. I have let her go, have no fear. I have released her; I only wish I could do the same for myself.'

Tom stood up and called out to the kind-faced man, 'I'm not a figment of your imagination, I am actually here.'

'Is that so,' said the voice. 'Well, that just shows you how far gone in madness I am. I actually thought I heard the echo of your ghostly little voice then. Tut, tut, silly old me, it looks like Ormestone has finally broken me. I feel like poor old pompous Humpty Dumpty, and sadly it seems that no one will ever be able to put me together again now either.'

'You're not mad,' said Tom. 'I really am here, I am just under an enchantment.'

'Of course you are,' said the voice, 'aren't we all.' And the scribe bent his head closer to Tom and peered at him through the big lenses of his glasses. 'Well, you certainly look real enough,' he said. 'Amazing the tricks that the mind can play after a while.'

'I'm no trick,' said Tom.

'Answering back too,' he said, 'whatever next, I wonder. I think I need a closer look at you.' He took his glasses off, and Tom noticed his sad-looking but friendly clear blue eyes. The man fished in a pocket and brought out a little square of cotton and began to polish the lenses of his glasses. Tom looked at the cloth and realized something with a shock. He stood stock still. He felt his heart beating faster. It was hammering in his little chest. Perhaps this man might know something about his father. How else would he have that particular piece of faded cotton, if he hadn't got it directly from him?

Tom fished in his bundle and pulled out the square of cotton that he had taken from the scarecrow's pocket. He laid it out as if it was a picnic blanket on the sheet of black notepaper. He smoothed it so that the heart pattern showed clearly. The man put his glasses back on and stared down at Tom and the cloth for a moment. Then he carefully put down his own little square of cotton next to the piece that Tom had laid down. They matched. The two little squares of Trueheart cotton lay side by side. One was a little more faded than the other, but they were undoubtedly cut from the same piece of cloth.

'I'm dreaming,' said the man, 'pinch me, you found one of my offcuts.'

'You're really not dreaming,' said Tom, and he moved closer to the man's face. 'You see I'm on a quest to stop a terrible invasion, and to rescue my older brothers. Well, that's one part of it, and the other thing is that I've also been looking for my father. He left home on an adventure when I was just a baby. That cloth is the family pattern. All adventurer families used to have their own pattern, you see, and we are the last of them, the adventuring families, that is. His name is Jack Trueheart, perhaps you might have met him somewhere on your travels?'

'Oh yes,' said the man quietly, 'I do remember meeting him. He was a very brave sort of fellow, very bold too, and so adventurous. He wouldn't have been content to sit in a stuffy library like this for ever, carrying out alchemical research experiments into the nature of sprite gold, and then just going quietly mad, rotting away, like some people I could mention. Do you know, just for an odd moment there I thought you were real, after all, and not just a piece of strictly forbidden wish fulfilment,' he said, and then sighed a very sad sigh.

'I *am* real, I am, I'm Tom Trueheart of the adventuring Truehearts. Please tell me everything you can remember about the man you met.'

'Tom,' whispered the man. 'So you're Tom, eh? A nice name, Tom. Little Tommy Thumb, little Tom, Tom, the piper's son, baby Tom.'

'Yes,' said Tom, 'that's right. As you can see I have been put under an enchantment by a sprite named Rumpelstiltskin; he works here like you. I thought I might be able to find a spell reversal in this library.'

'Rumpelstiltskin did this to you?' the man asked quietly.

'Yes. Back in our Land of Stories, this awful Ormestone abducted all my older brothers and their princess brides and on their big wedding day too. Rumpelstiltskin shrunk me down, and then Ormestone brought them all here in his airship and I followed.'

'You followed?'

'Yes.'

'You're a brave little figment then?'

The man extended his finger out towards Tom and laid it on the page of his notebook. 'Pinch me,' he said. 'No, really, go on, don't be shy, pinch me, pinch me as hard as you can.'

'Really?'

'Really.'

Tom walked across the notebook page to where the man's index finger lay. He stepped up and grabbed the soft part, the pad of the forefinger, and squeezed it as hard as he possibly could.

'Ouch,' said the man, and Tom looked up and saw the man open his eyes and a single magnified tear well up behind the lens of the man's glasses.

'Sorry,' said Tom, 'I didn't mean to hurt you, but you did say as hard as you can.'

'No need to say sorry. I'm pleased to meet you properly at last, young Tom,' he said in a very quiet voice.

'And I am pleased to meet you too,' said Tom cheerfully. 'So tell me all about how you met my father?'

'Well, I didn't really meet him,' said the man. 'You see, Tom, I think I *am* your father.'

Chapter 36

Jollity landed at the base of the tower. He perched on a ledge set in the wall and took his bearings. He had passed various bridges that led from the tower into the huge main body of the castle. He had seen no sign of Tom, and he had to assume and hope that Tom had at least found his way down one of the many corridors to hide himself away.

Outside he could hear the drum beats and bugles of the Dark Army, the skeleton hordes. They were surely right outside the castle now. He flew up to a higher ledge nearby which had an arrow-slit window opening above it and peered through. Below the granite crag, in the dark land surrounding the castle, Jollity could see an encampment. Tents and bivouacs, flapping black flags, and burning fires stretched away into the distance across the plain. Snow was falling; it was a bleak sight. Clouds of crows and bats were flying around among the tents.

A door slammed somewhere just below Jollity, and Ormestone himself appeared. He swished along with the stitched-faced man and a tall booted skeleton wearing a black cloak and an iron helmet. They swept into a chamber and Jollity left Tom's sword on the ledge and followed them. He arrived at a tall door with the words ENDING HALL lettered across it in the shivery greenish-white lettering.

Jollity landed and went up close to the door. It was hugely tall and the top ended in a pointed arch, just like the windows in the old palace. The door stood slightly open and Jollity crept in through the gap. The hall was in almost total darkness. A cold blue fire was burning in the huge fireplace.

In the centre of the big empty chamber stood a huge weighing scale, and next to that were some sprites and beside them a pile of heavy looking filled sacks. Gold, thought Jollity. Sprite gold, too, I'll bet. Ormestone sat on his throne near the fire and the skeleton stood beside him, the reflected blue light of the fire flickering across his head. The stitched-faced man picked up one of the big sacks and heaved it across to the scales. Jollity watched from the shadows as the sacks of gold were taken one by one and put on to the scales to be weighed. The various weights were called out and then written down. It took a long time to weigh all the sacks. Finally the skeleton was shown the resulting total. It examined the sheets of black paper, tracing its bony finger down the columns of figures.

It shook its skull. 'Not enough,' was all it said in a dry cracked voice that seemed to have come from somewhere deep underground, 'not enough.' It began to march down the hall away from Ormestone, its red eyes blazing.

'Wait,' Ormestone said, 'I can add more, I can find more.'

The skeleton stopped. 'An amount was agreed,' it replied, 'there should be exactly that amount, no more and no less.'

'We are so close. There is such a tiny shortfall, the minutest difference, can we not proceed in any case?'

The skeleton turned on its boot heel and came up close to Ormestone. It reached out a skeleton hand and grabbed him by the collar of his cloak.

'The exact amount, exact,' it said, glaring into Ormestone's face with its red eyes. 'So the story plan was written, and agreed, and we shall live the story as written, tomorrow morning, sharp.'

The skeleton swept out of the hall past the hidden figure of Jollity. Ormestone followed after the skeleton, calling out, 'Tomorrow, oh yes, the exact amount will be here tomorrow.'

Jollity watched as Ormestone set off down the dark corridor, his face set like a mask. Ormestone had the list of gold totals in his hand and he went straight back round the spiral of corridor flanked by two of his wolves until he reached the sprite-guarded door. Jollity flew on and hid himself a little higher up in the tower with a view of the door.

Tom stood very still looking up at the man's kindly face. His features were strong. This man could indeed be the father to any of the Jacks. He did wear his hair long, a little like a Viking warrior's. His hands certainly looked strong too.

'I don't understand, I—' said Tom, but he was interrupted by the door crashing open. Ormestone, and two bleary sprites and two wolves, burst into the library.

Tom quickly dived beneath the edge of the book. He could barely keep still, and his heart was bursting; suppose this man really was his father?

'Well,' said Ormestone, 'your usefulness is fast approaching its end. If there are still no results then I am afraid it will be the end for you, and, of course, for all of your kind.'

'Your majesty,' the man looked up and took a deep breath, 'I feel that I have made real progress but so far I have not seen the physical results from my last attempt, which must be finishing very soon. I have nothing solid to show for it yet, but I do feel I was getting somewhere near.'

'I see,' said Ormestone. 'Really, this is your last chance. It turns out that there is a shortfall, a tiny and minute shortfall. It means insufficient funds for my Army of Darkness. Even a minute fraction of sprite gold would be enough. Let us hope it has worked this time, for your sake, or I shall be forced to feed you and all of the rest of your kind to my hungry wolves. As you know, that is the kind of ending that I like to see. Right, come on, we must go and see right now, the general will be at the gate at dawn for his gold.' The wolves stepped forward, low growls in their throats.

'Let me just finish writing up this last calculation here, sire, and then we will go to the furnace together and see what has happened since I was last there,' the man said. 'If there should be a result it would be a crime not to have kept an exact record of how it has worked.'

'One minute then and no more,' said Ormestone impatiently. 'Hurry up and get on with it.'

The man wrote a few more words on his sheet of black paper, blotted it with a sifter, and blew off the surplus. Then he stood and shrugged himself into a dark coat, picked up his piece of glasses cloth from the papers in front of him, and allowed himself to be nudged and pushed out of the room by the two wolves. The sprites slammed the door and Tom was left alone. He crept out from under the book. He was in a daze. His head was spinning. He was not sure if had just met his long-lost father or not. He was in a state of shock.

He had no memory of a fond face to go on, there was just the little picture at home of his father in his full adventurer's armour, and that would have been painted a long time ago. He tried to think back to that picture, tried to imagine it and match it up to the man he had just met. He couldn't see either of them clearly in his head, all was now vague and a muddle.

He looked down at his feet. He was standing on the piece of paper that the man had made his last written entry on. Tom started to read what was written, almost absently. He walked along the paper looking at all the columns and numbers and symbols. The strange line of figures ran out and he saw that at the end of the last column there was a note, and it was a note addressed to him.

He read, *'Tom, follow me, I am being taken to the Furnace Building, which is outside and behind the main castle. Stay close, and be brave, and always with a true heart, Dad.'*

Tom sat down next to his own little square of Trueheart cotton, his head still reeling. His own father, his missing dad; could it really have been him, or was it some terrible trick staged by Ormestone?

Tom stood and picked up the Trueheart cloth and put it back carefully into his bundle. He climbed down the table leg, keeping a close eye out for spiders and any stray filaments of web. He rolled under the door and was soon out in the corridor again. He made his way back to the bridge and halfway across he heard the beating of wings. He froze. He imagined that a bat or a rogue sentinel crow was about to attack him. The shadow of a bird crossed the stonework of the bridge. Tom looked up and saw with relief that it was only Jollity the crow. The bird landed on the bridge, and Tom could see that his own sword was held firmly in the bird's beak. Jollity dropped the sword on to the stone.

'There you are at last, Tom, I've been looking for you.'

Tom ran across the bridge and picked up his sword, and it sparked once, as he tucked it into his scabbard.

'Something amazing might have just happened,' Tom said. 'I can't explain now, Jollity, but we must go to a building behind the main castle right away.' He climbed on to Jollity's back.

'Hold on then, Tom,' said Jollity.

Halfway down the staircase Ormestone was waylaid by a sentinel crow. The crow stood on the stair below a window.

'Your majesty,' it said.

'Yes, what is it, I am very busy,' Ormestone said.

'There has been a sighting, sire.'

'Where?'

'In the woods. The princesses have been seen travelling all together.'

'Is that so?' said Ormestone. 'Right, go with this goblin, show him where, and all will be dealt with once and for all. Go then, my friend,' he added to the goblin, 'and do your worst,' Ormestone said with a chuckle.

Chapter 37

The princesses hugged each of the swans in turn, wrapping their arms around the long white necks. Each princess hugged each swan, so that they would be sure of having hugged their beloved at least once before they set off on their dangerous mission.

The swans made mournful honking noises as the girls gathered themselves, checking their swords and bits of armour. Jack stood by the horse and cart and the horse swished her mane and tail proudly. The princesses were to set off first through the woods on foot. Jack was to set off as if to market with the swans on the cart. They were to rendezvous as near to the castle as they could get given the skeleton army and their position.

The swans set up a great noise as the princesses all walked away one after the other and disappeared among the trees.

Jack tried to calm the swans; he patted each one on the head. 'We'll see them all again soon enough, boys,' he said. 'I'll look after you now, don't worry. Into the cart with you.'

The woodcutter was worn out with carrying the ungrateful sprite on her back, and her husband was worn out with trying to keep up.

'Can't you go any faster?' said the sprite. 'I really must get to the castle soon.'

'To be honest, your little lordship, I can't, I'm fair worn out with it all.'

'Well, I suppose I'm a little more rested than I would have been,' said the sprite. 'Oh, but I must find my beauties, my loves.' He promptly hopped off on to the ground, and stretched his arms out.

The woodcutter caught her breath, and the

woodcutter's husband eventually caught up with them.

'Having a rest, dear? Quite right too,' he said.

'No,' said the sprite, 'we're just not going fast enough; I need to get to the king right away. Now you are supposed to be a woodcutter, go and choose me a good stout hazel stick about yay high and some birch twigs and hurry up about it.'

'Why on earth would you want—?'

'No time for any silly questions. I need a broom, just do it now and hurry please.'

'Very well, sir.'

The woodcutter set to work, grumbling under her breath. She deftly fashioned a passable looking besom broom with the twigs and then the woodcutter's husband was made to trim the birch twigs until they were even.

'There,' said the woodcutter.

'It'll do,' said the sprite coldly, and he stepped over the broom, tucked up his cloak, pointed his little stick at the broom and then suddenly took off from the ground, hovering at head height.

'Thank you for all your efforts, but now I fear we must part.'

'My, my,' spluttered the woodcutter's husband. 'I

knew it, you are some sort of wood sprite.'

The sprite interrupted him. 'How very observant,' he said coldly.

'What about our reward, our wish?' the woodcutter called out.

'Never trust a sprite in the woods,' the little man called back and took off, high above the trees, and was soon gone.

'So much for our bird in the hand,' said the wood-cutter's husband, as he watched the sprite soar away over the dark trees towards the castle.

'Never mind all that,' whispered the woodcutter. 'Looks like our other wish might still be on the cards,' and she pointed to the clearing ahead where Jack Trueheart could surely be seen trotting towards them on their own horse and cart. Her husband reached into his bag and pulled out the big old duelling pistol.

Tom and Jollity landed on the roof of a tall rough-cast building. It was built on a narrow pointed mound of rock which rose out of the deep abyss that surrounded the castle. The building was joined to the main part of the castle by a rickety looking bridge. There was a tall chimney belching dark smoke, and the pointed roof felt warm, and here the snow was fast melting in patches across the tiles. Tom looked down into the building through a dormer window.

Inside was all red light and heat. Tom could see figures, and a huge metal furnace which took up most of the space. There was a bench to one side of the furnace with glass flasks, a set of scales, deep stone bowls, retorts, and other alchemical equipment scattered all over it.

'That's the man from the library,' said Tom. 'I talked to him. He had a section of Trueheart cloth, and he says he is my father.'

'Your father,' said Jollity, 'are you sure?'

'No, I'm not sure, but I feel something very strange inside.'

As they watched, a servant sprite poured something bright and molten from a hot container into a stone bowl. Ormestone turned a timing glass and then watched and waited as the sand slipped through. When the bowl had cooled Ormestone and the man from the library probed the contents. Ormestone shook his head. He picked up the bowl and threw it across the chamber, where it smashed against the wall.

'Useless,' he said, 'useless. Give me one good reason why I should not feed you to my wolves this minute. Months you have had since I bargained you away from that place, and what have you repaid me with, nothing. You are worse than useless. You not only killed my first giant, but your hideous sons conspired to ruin all my earlier story plans. It shall not happen again. I have taken steps to ensure that they will trouble me no further. I repeat, give me one good reason why you should be allowed to live. Well?'

The man panicked. 'I think I know what went wrong, your majesty, from studying my notes. I will just need a little more time. Give me another hour or so and I am sure I will succeed this time.'

'You will have one half of one hour. I need my speck, my sliver of sprite gold, my final weight and then everything can begin properly. This is your final chance to make it, there will not be another.'

There came a hammering on the door. Ormestone opened it and stepped out on to the terrace. A servant sprite stood at the door with Rumpelstiltskin.

'Well, well, well, what have we here?' Ormestone said coldly.

'Why, your humble servant, sire,' said Rumpelstiltskin, bowing low. 'I went to the gold mine, master, your highness, and I can report that all the gold was gathered in.'

'I know that, it is old news indeed. The gold was delivered here, smelted, refined, weighed, measured, what of it?'

'I lined up the Trueheart brothers,' he carried on, 'outside the goblin mine and I dealt with them for you, once and for all. I carried out a transformation. Five of them are fully transformed,' he said, 'the sixth I am afraid escaped by chance.'

'Transformed to what?' Ormestone asked impatiently.

'As swans, your majesty. It was one of the story starts we found, "The Six Swan Brothers", I thought I would use it as an ending.'

Ormestone opened his slit of a mouth wide and laughed a horrible chilling laugh.

'Perhaps you have just redeemed yourself, after all.

Something you may do for me for old times' sake. Shackle and cage the fool in there so he cannot leave until I wish him to. Otherwise you may consider yourself dismissed, back to your woodland hovel with you. You might like to know that I have sent my *new* assistant out into those same woods to deal with those troublesome princesses once and for all.'

A flash of anger and agony suddenly blazed in what remained of the little sprite's heart. He would have his revenge now.

He went into the furnace room and raised his arms. There was a flash of light and a series of large iron bars appeared, snapped, and clanged to in sections around the man from the library. They covered his bench and all around the entrance to the furnace. The wolf stood guard outside the caged area. Rumpelstiltskin swept out of the furnace room and scuttled off, his job finally done. He was no longer the favourite of his master. His master was no longer a favourite of his. He set out to wreak his revenge, and set off as fast as he could for the woods.

Jollity, with Tom on his back, flew down quietly from the window and between the bars of the cage into the hot chamber below. He floated down silently and came to a halt, landing quietly on the table in the shadows among all the retorts and bowls. Tom stepped off and crept about among all the mysterious equipment. The man from the library was busy with a pestle and mortar, tipping things in, and crushing, and stirring. He was so intent on what he was doing that he barely seemed aware of the cage that had sprung up around him. The wolf had settled down with its head drooping on its paws, pressed against the outside of the bars, basking in the radiant heat from the furnace. It would soon be fast asleep.

'You read my note then?' said the man quietly.

Tom crept out from behind a stone bowl. 'How did you know I was here?' he said.

'I saw you flying down on your crow.'

'Yes, this is Jollity; we travelled here together.'

'Hello, Jollity,' said the man.

'Hello,' said Jollity. 'Tom, a word,' and the bird nodded his beak to indicate that they should go behind one of the retorts.

'I don't know what to think, Tom. Part of me wants to believe that he is telling you the truth, and yet . . . '

'I know,' said Tom, 'I feel the same.'

'Keep talking to him and maybe the truth will emerge either way.'

Tom stepped back into view. 'Sorry,' he said.

'No, Tom, you are right to be suspicious of me, but I have urgent problems here. I must make a small quantity of sprite gold or suffer a terrible fate, along with your brothers apparently.'

'You can make gold then?' said Tom.

'Not really, no. I told Ormestone that I could, and because of that he got me away from a terrible situation. It's a long story and one for another time. You see I once knew some elves and they showed me a certain kind of sprite gold from a distant mountain in the Land of Myths and Legends. They said there was a way of actually making that gold from a secret formula. They gave me one of their special little gold buttons. I mounted it on a pin and put it away somewhere at home. It's probably been lost by now. I told Ormestone that I knew their secret, anything to get away from what was likely to happen to me. I've been forced to study alchemy and try to make it work for him ever since.'

Tom suddenly remembered something. He took his

bundle from his shoulder and tipped the contents out on to the table. Among the scraps and tatters, among all the little lengths of twine, something tiny glinted gold in the warm light from the open furnace door. It was the little button that Tom's mother had given him to travel with as a memento of his father. He held it up.

'I brought this with me because it was something that Mum said might have belonged to my father, to . . . I mean . . . to you,' Tom said in wonder, looking up at the friendly face above him.

The man took the little pin and button and looked at it closely. 'Why, that's it, Tom,' he said. 'The very thing, and very fine sprite gold it is too. I just need to melt this down and reshape it and that fiend will finally have his proof, and even perhaps his gold total, complete.'

He busied himself with a crucible and tongs. He put the button in the furnace and then he carefully tipped the molten drips into one of the stone moulds. They waited together for it to cool while the wolf slept on the floor.

'How is your mother then, Tom?' he whispered.

'She's all right. She gets a bit fed up with the noise

when everyone is at home, all the Jacks banging their quarterstaffs on the stairs, you know, that sort of thing. She was looking forward to the weddings.'

'Your brothers were all in good shape then?'

'Oh yes, they were all right. Five of them have met these princesses, and they were getting married when that Ormestone burst into the ceremony and brought them all here and now, well, they have been turned into swans. We are going to do something about that, don't worry.'

'I am sure you will, Tom, this is a place of wonders, after all. It's been a long time since I've seen you, Tom,' he said, 'and do you know something funny: you were bigger on the day I left home, than you are now.'

'I know,' said Tom, 'like I said, I have to find a way to restore my size, to reverse this spell.'

'There will be a way for all these wonders to be reversed, Tom, all will be well,' the man said and smiled.

'You really are my dad, aren't you?' said Tom suddenly. 'I only half believed it before, but it's true, isn't it?'

'Yes, it's true, Tom, I really am.'

'Dad,' said Tom, staring up in amazement.

'Tom,' said his father, smiling down at him and nodding. 'At last, my boy, I—'

The door crashed open and Ormestone burst in with three wolves. The guard wolf stretched its legs out and shook its head. Tom hid behind the jars and scales and pots on the bench.

'Well?' Ormestone said as he opened the iron cage.

'I think that it has finally worked, look.' And the man held out the little mould with the gold in it triumphantly.

'Well well, so it has. My, what an asset you finally turn out to be. I can pay the Army of Darkness, after all. I can invade and destroy your ridiculous land. You have made it all possible with just this one tiny little fragment, ha ha.' He took the gold. 'Come, you shall witness my triumph.'

The wolves nudged Tom's father out of the cage and out of the furnace room. Finally Tom crept out of his hiding place.

'Come on, Jollity, we must do something to stop all this and rescue him.'

'Indeed we must,' said Jollity. 'But what?'

341

The princesses walked carefully through the dark woods towards the castle. They finally emerged from the woods onto the scrubby plain. Black tents were pitched all across and fires smouldered. They kept to the tree line and made their way around the edge of the encampment. A crow flew near them and then came back again and followed them, flying through the trees at a low height. Zinnia spotted it.

'Look, isn't that Jollity the crow?'

'See if it talks to us; Tom's crow could talk,' said Rapunzel.

'Can you talk?' asked Snow White.

'Who's asking?' said the bird.

'We are.'

'Who's we?'

'*We* are we,' said Snow White imperiously, 'as you well know; you only flew off with Tom an hour or so ago. I am Snow White, you silly bird, and this is Princess Zinnia, this is Cinderella, this is Sleeping Beauty, and this is Rapunzel. We are on our way to the Dark Castle.'

'Ah,' said the bird slyly, 'that's right, of course, just follow me.'

So the princesses followed the bird along dark secret paths that took them past the army encampment and right up near the mound of the sinister castle itself. As they walked they were followed secretly from a little way behind by Rumpelstiltskin, who every now and then sighed and muttered the words, 'Oh, my beauties,' or, 'Oh, so beautiful,' under his breath.

Chapter 38

An hour or so before, Jack was trotting along with the good-natured horse and the cart full of his swan brothers. He kept an eye on the surrounding woods for the army but so far the road was clear and every so often he clicked a reassuring sound to the horse, as they carried on down the path.

Then suddenly the woodcutter, with her trusty axe across her shoulders, stepped out from the trees on to the path right in front of Jack and the horse and cart. The horse shied, her front legs went up and Jack tumbled to the ground. The swans flew up honking and then quickly settled again and began hissing from inside the cart. The woodcutter's husband stood over Jack.

'I am arresting you for the theft of our horse and cart,' he said, 'and numerous other crimes.'

'Don't be daft,' said Jack. 'I told you, you shall have the horse back soon enough, I am just on my way to market with these here swans.'

'Think again,' said the man, brandishing his old-fashioned heavy duelling pistol. He pointed it at Jack with a shaking hand. 'This is cocked, primed, and loaded,' he said, 'and I won't hesitate to use it. There's a generous reward out for handing you in at the castle.'

'Careful now with that,' said Jack, 'you could take an eye out. I know all about your so-called king. You'll get nothing from him, his promises are as hollow as he is,' he said standing up and rubbing his bottom where he had hit the path.

'He will grant us a wish, and that is rare.'

The woodcutter dragged the reluctant horse, pulling the cart full of angry swans behind her. The horse held her head low, snorted and shook her mane.

'Come on then, dear,' the woodcutter said, 'we've no time to lose. Our wonderful reward awaits us, and it looks like we've got the bonus of a nice cartload of swans to sell at the market.' The swans hissed at her as the little procession set off through the trees towards the castle.

'Don't see many of those bad-tempered birds hereabouts in this country,' said the husband looking back at the five white birds in the cart. 'I think they're an omen of some sort, for sure.'

'Oh, they're an omen all right,' Jack muttered, nodding quickly at the horse, which had turned round to look at him as the swans hissed on.

On the edge of a field crowded with tall poles and cartwheels and skeletons the crow which was leading the princesses suddenly flew up and vanished into the air, landing on one of the wheels. A nasty looking grey goblin stepped out from behind a tree. He clicked his fingers with a smile on his face. A skeleton instantly appeared beside him, with a sword in its hand. It turned to the princesses with its red eyes and let out what sounded like a battle cry, and at that sound other armed skeletons soon appeared, one after the other. Some shimmied down from the poles and walked towards the princesses. The crow was, of course, not Tom's crow after all, but a servant of the dreaded Ormestone and it had led them into this terrible trap. The princesses formed a tight circle. More skeletons in black cloaks strode out from the edge of the forest.

'Weapons at the ready, girls,' Rapunzel said.

'We'll take some of them with us, at least,' said Snow White, waving an axe.

'They're only old bones and sprite power,' said Sleeping Beauty.

'We are doing this for the Trueheart brothers,' said Princess Zinnia.

'And we do it with a true heart,' said Cinderella. 'I'm used to getting my hands dirty, come on.'

The princesses moved forward as a group, their weapons held out in front of them. Rapunzel broke ranks, ran forward, and despatched the first skeleton with a swift blow from the Master's sword. The red light died in the creature's eyes as it tumbled to the floor in a heap. Snow White was dealt a fast blow with a sword, which glanced off her armour and she turned and quickly beheaded the nearest skeleton or two with one sweeping movement of her sword. Rapunzel ran at a group of skeletons, pushed them over with her shield, held them down, and despatched them one by one.

The princesses found it relatively easy to destroy the skeletons. They seemed to have little fight, or courage, or guile, in them; they were like puppets that simply crumpled once the strings were broken. The princesses fought their way across the field back towards the cover of the trees, slashing, fencing, lunging, at the melee of armed skeletons. Skulls rolled, or flew up in the air, swords and shields flashed in the morning light, and hundreds of red eyes bore down on them. The goblin, seeing that his work was done, scampered back towards the castle. He was smiling a broad and nasty smile to himself.

The princesses were surely about to be overwhelmed by the sheer numbers of armed skeletons, when all the lights in the skeletons' eyes suddenly blinked out into darkness, and the skeletons stopped moving altogether. They all folded in on themselves as if they had just run out of energy and stopped. One fell at Rapunzel's feet. She kicked out at it. It lay still on the ground, grinning up at her.

'What on earth?' she said, and looked around at the surrounding skeletons. All were now frozen in their positions across the field. Some stood at odd angles to one another, some lay slumped on the ground. A dark cloud of crows suddenly swooped down and flew over them. A cold wind swept across the field suddenly along with their shadows over the scrubby grass.

'Extraordinary,' said Snow White.

'What happened?' asked Cinderella.

'I really don't know,' said Rapunzel, 'but we shouldn't hang around here just to find out. That crow led us into a trap, and there will be plenty more of those skeleton things soon enough. Come on, time to go to the castle right now.'

They set off leaving the heaps of bones just where

they lay. Moments later Rumpelstiltskin emerged quietly from the trees behind them. He now had a trophy of fresh green leaves on his head. He muttered to himself as he picked his way among the stalled skeletons. 'Oh, my lovelies, my beautiful princesses.' He settled down among the heaps of bones on the ground and said, 'Ah, my brave, brave, beautiful girls, now I have saved you.'

He let too much time pass sitting and gloating over his secret victory. The princesses soon met another group of hundreds of skeleton soldiers on the road, and they were easily arrested and taken in a line back towards the castle and their fate.

Chapter 39

The stitched-faced man stood beside the big scales which he had lugged and dragged out on to the terrace at the front of the Dark Castle. The gold was all piled up in a tall mound. The sprite gold was so warm in colour, it looked almost alive, beautiful even as the bleak early light flickered over it. Black flags flapped and cracked in the cold wind. Skeleton soldiers lined the mound's edge above the deep abyss that surrounded the castle.

The drawbridge was down and a collection of local peasants on their way to market in their drab-coloured clothes had been bullied, cajoled, charmed, and threatened over the drawbridge onto the mound just after dawn. They had come to witness the great gold ceremony and to see the Dark Army and the beginning of the spread of the new era of unhappy endings for all, everywhere.

The king's big black airship was tethered to one of the tall tower pinnacles of the castle, its skull and crossbones glaring down on the event, while the murder of crows swarmed around it. Among the peasants waiting for the ceremony to begin were the woodcutter and her husband with Jack and the horse and cart and the cargo of angry swans.

'It's odd to see such clean looking white birds in this place,' said one peasant.

'Aren't they more usually seen in romantic stories with love and princes and such?' whispered another.

'Perhaps they've lost their way, poor things?' opined a third.

The stitched-faced man glared down at the crowd with his huge arms folded across his chest. Then the drumbeats started. Regular muffled thumps of the bass drum and then the skeleton buglers blew a ragged fanfare. Ormestone walked out on to the high terrace, while beside him walked the skeleton general in his full regalia. A half hearted cheer went up from the peasants. The stitched-faced man raised his arms up as if to say 'louder' and the weary crowd roared their approval again only with a little more forced enthusiasm.

Hidden among the crowd was the dark figure of Rumpelstiltskin. He still wore his circlet of fresh green leaves on his head, and he held the little length of twisted twig discreetly in his hand.

Tom and the crow flew quietly in low circles around the castle mound. Tom clung to Jollity as low as he could, partly to avoid being seen, and partly because of the cold. The closer he was in among the feathers, then the warmer he was too. When Ormestone appeared and the crowd cheered politely, Jollity glided down with his wings outstretched and landed not far from the cart and Jack and the swans.

Jack was patting the carthorse kindly and reassuringly on the neck, and was standing wedged between the grumpy looking husband and the tall, cross looking woodcutter who had her axe over her shoulder. He looked around the crowd but there was no sign yet of the princesses. He hoped that they were biding their time.

A fanfare rang out and Ormestone stepped forward to the very edge of the terrace. He raised his arms, there was silence, and he was about to speak when the bold and angry woodcutter woman called out very loudly into the hush: 'Look here, your majesty, we've caught him, the one you were looking for. We had both of them once, but one of them got away from us. This one here stole our horse and cart and we are here to claim our reward, your majesty.' And they pushed Jack forward.

Ormestone looked out into the crowd, and he saw an odd group: the slightly intimidating figure of a tall woman with an axe, one of the Trueheart brothers, the bumpkin one who belonged in a farmyard, and a small older man behind him holding a large dangerous looking old duelling pistol in one hand and the reins of a recently unharnessed and disgruntled looking carthorse in the other. Now this was just the sort of thing Ormestone wanted to see and hear.

'Well, well,' said Ormestone as benignly as he could, 'look at this, what have we here? Come forward, all of you, don't be shy. Now you stand just there and tell me your name.'

'I am Mrs Woodcutter, sire, and this is my husband Mr Woodcutter.'

'Welcome to you both. I see that you have caught the notorious wish-fulfiller and would-be adventurer Jack Trueheart?'

'Yes, sir,' said the old man. 'He chanced upon us in the forest when we were on our way here with another wish fulfilment to hand in to you, a very tiny enchanted boy.'

'That would be me,' Tom whispered to Jollity.

'Oh, I know that one,' said Ormestone. 'You were quite right to try and turn them in, do carry on.'

'This one stole our trusty horse here and our best cart over there too.'

The horse whinnied and shook her mane. The swans hissed in the cart, and several peasants nearby stepped one pace away. 'They can break an arm with one blow of those wings,' said one.

'We always wanted a son to help us in our forest work but we were not blessed,' said the woodcutter. 'We thought you might grant us such a wish seeing as we found and brought you your fugitive,' and she bowed low.

'Do you know,' said Ormestone, 'I am in the mood to do just that,' and he gestured at the heap of glittering gold. 'I am in a very good mood and it may well be that I shall actually grant you a wish through the offices of my assistant, who should be somewhere here.'

'Oh, thank you, your majesty,' the woodcutter said.

'If you would all wait just over there, because later I have a surprise to reveal. First I think it is time to get on and pay the Army of Darkness for their forthcoming invasion of the Land of Stories.'

The stitched-faced man raised his arms and the crowd dutifully cheered again.

Jack stood fuming next to the horse. He was biding his time, waiting for the decisive moment to act. The little sprite Rumpelstiltskin, mingled as he was with the crowd, waited for his own special moment. It was plain that the new assistant was expecting to do some sprite magic for his master. Well, Rumpelstiltskin was not easily thwarted and he had some magic of his own to do.

There was a flurry suddenly in the crowd. Skeleton

soldiers advanced pushing some girls, five of them, and they were marched swiftly across the drawbridge.

'Well now,' said Ormestone, 'look here, everybody. The skeleton army have found my five so-called princesses from that other place. That sad island far from here where they encourage happy endings. Here they come, the lovely Zinnia, the wondrous Snow White, the marvellous Sleeping Beauty, the pretty Cinderella, and the fearsome Rapunzel, so nice of you all to come to my ceremony. Of course, as I was good enough to come to yours, it seems only fair that you should come to mine, and also let's not forget how clever you are at spinning.'

The goblin assistant appeared and followed the girls across the drawbridge, and Jack felt his heart lurch. 'Chain them,' Ormestone said. The goblin raised his grey green arms and pointed at the princesses, and sudden chains linked them all together.

'We must do something now,' Tom said.

'Wait, Tom,' said Jollity, 'wait, our moment will come.'

Somewhere in the crowd a very quiet voice said, 'Oh no, my lovelies, oh, my poor darlings.'

The five white swans flapped their wings angrily

and hissed, and then settled and watched, and waited.

Ormestone drew a sword out from under his black cloak. 'This sword is almost as powerful as the ceremonial sword of the Story Bureau, very nearly its equal, and was forged and refined by the same masterly hand. Once I have paid my army their due I thought we might have an old-fashioned *really* unhappy ending, a public beheading or six, one boy, five girls. No wait, better still, we can have seven beheadings, a proper fairy tale number, sevens and threes, never twos and sixes, eh?' A big cheer went up from the skeleton army, and a shocked gasp from the peasants.

'Now,' said Ormestone, 'the all important weighing of the gold.'

The heaps of gold had been added to the scales by the stitched-faced man. The balance pointer was almost in the middle. The skeleton general stepped forward and studied the balance.

'Still short,' he growled, turning his glowing red eyes to Ormestone.

Ormestone produced from under his robe the little tiny gold button that had been melted and moulded in the furnace room. He added it to the heap of gold and then the balance read dead level: it was the exact amount. The stitched-faced man raised his arms and the peasants cheered again.

The skeleton general nodded his grim satisfaction.

The skeleton army raised their arms as one and let out another rattling cheer. There was a moment of quiet as Ormestone beamed at his great success, and then a grating voice broke the mood.

'Excuse me, what about our reward then, your highness?' said the woodcutter impatiently.

'Oh yes,' said Ormestone, the smile fading from his face, 'your reward. A wish fulfilled was it not. Now, tell me how many wishes have you had in the past if any? And be honest now,' said Ormestone.

'Two, your majesty,' said the old man with the pistol, 'if you count the little boy who turned up at our door.'

'Ssh, you old fool,' said the woodcutter.

'No, he is right to be truthful,' said Ormestone. 'So then, you have but the one wish left, and what shall it be? You have only to tell my friend the goblin here and it shall be granted.'

'Well, your majesty,' the woodcutter began.

Her husband interrupted her. 'Sire, your majesty, I

cannot keep this hidden for any longer. I am afraid that we once wished for something in a very wrong way indeed. We wished that the very poor, but very pretty, peasant girl who lived near us in the dark forest should be transformed into a horse—'

Now his wife interrupted him. 'Don't listen to him, your majesty. We met a little goblin, just like your assistant here, out in the wood once who granted us the wish of a very useful horse, but I would have preferred a son to help me really.'

'So you are telling me that you wished for this poor girl, this woodland neighbour, to be changed into a useful horse to help you in your work?' said Ormestone raising his arms for silence.

'Yes, your highness,' said the woodcutter's husband.

Ormestone laughed his cruel laugh. 'Well,' he said, 'you are certainly living in the right place. You are both as dark as can be. Your wish is granted ha ha.'

The goblin stepped further forward, and bowed a little.

The woodcutter gasped. 'But, sire, your majesty, this is the very goblin himself.'

'Then it is only right that he should be the one to

enhance the enchantment and complete your wish for a son,' said Ormestone with a chuckle.

The goblin pointed over at the carthorse.

From among the crowd the little sprite Rumpelstiltskin pointed his stick wand at the exact same moment. There was a searing flash from the stage, the horse whinnied and a cloud of dramatic dark purple smoke filled the terrace. When the smoke cleared, where the horse had stood next to Jack and the old man with the pistol, there now stood a beautiful young peasant girl, and where the goblin had been standing there stood a proper solid dappled-grey carthorse. The peasant crowd cheered wildly, it had been a brilliant trick.

'How very amusing,' said Ormestone, puzzled. 'Well, it looks to me, madam, I am afraid, as if it is more of an unhappy ending for you. Just another work horse, no son and heir after all. And that was your third wish.'

The woodcutter looked shocked, as did her husband.

Jack looked at the girl standing next to him. He was shocked too, but also there was a strange sense of recognition. There was something familiar about this girl, though he had never seen her before.

The girl smiled at him. 'Hello, Jack, I am Jill,' she

said quietly. 'I was a miserable and enchanted carthorse until just a moment ago. Those two had me transformed into a horse to work for them.'

Jack felt as if lightning had struck him in his heart; he was suddenly filled to the brim with love for this girl, this Jill. Jill raised her arm and whacked Jack hard across his bottom.

'Ow,' said Jack.

'That's for paddling my flanks when I was a horse,' she said, laughing good-naturedly.

Two guards, on Ormestone's orders, came and took Jack over to the centre of the stage.

Ormestone narrowed his eyes, something very odd was going on. 'Bring out that other Trueheart quickly, let's make up the seven.'

Tom's father was suddenly fetched out from the castle, and the moment he appeared on the terrace Jack fell to his knees in shock and the swans all flew up and circled in the air, calling out and honking.

Tom held on to Jollity that bit tighter. 'Wait, Tom,' said Jollity, 'we will have our chance soon, I am sure.'

Ormestone ordered the princesses to be brought

forward too. They were pulled out in a long line across the terrace, with their heads bowed. Ormestone walked in front of them with the sword in his hand.

'A fine group of pretty heads to take back to the Land of Stories. They shall adorn my first banquet table, five heads of five princesses, and with them later, five delicious roast swans. Ha ha, yes, I know all about you swans.'

He stood to his full scarecrow height and aimed his sword first at Rapunzel. There was a sudden flash of light on the terrace behind him, a great flash and glow just where the pile of sprite gold stood on the balance scale. When the glow faded, instead of the mound of gold there was now a great haystack-shaped pile of drab-coloured straw.

A chill wind blew suddenly across the terrace and began to scatter the straw in the air. It blew every-where, drifted about among the crowd. The peasants grasped at it.

'Look, it's just straw,' they cried out, 'it's not gold at all.'

Ormestone dropped the sword in shock. He ran to the dwindling straw stack and plunged his skinny scarecrow arms in among the scattering fragments. 'No,' he cried, 'my gold, my lovely gold no, no, no.' He sobbed and wailed while the peasants laughed.

The chains snapped away from the princesses, and the five swans all landed on the terrace. All around as far as could be seen most of the skeleton army suddenly collapsed to the ground, just as they had on the field, like a set of puppets after the strings have been cut. Many of them tumbled over into the deep dark abyss around the castle.

Tom and the crow flew up and over at once to the terrace, and no sooner had they landed than the few remaining skeletons waded in among the princesses, and a battle started. The peasants, sensing real danger now, panicked, and the jostling crowd fled across the drawbridge.

Ormestone ran back from his diminishing pile of wind-blown worthless straw. He picked up the sword, and waved it in his bony hands. Tom and the crow flew up, Tom pulled out his own sword, and it flashed with light. The woodcutter's husband was quickly knocked down by Jack who grabbed the duelling pistol from him.

The woodcutter quickly mounted the new carthorse that had once been a goblin, and clopped over to her husband. 'Come on,' she said, 'quick, let's cut our losses and head back to the forest, this kind of thing's not for us, husband.' She helped her husband up on to the horse which protested with an angry whinny and a shake of its dappled-grey head and then they set off home on the back of their new and last wish-fulfilment.

'You'll need to build a good new cart later; we can't go on like this, husband,' said the woodcutter.

'Of course, dearest,' her husband answered, ducking to dodge a blow from an enraged skeleton.

Soon the terrace was full of fighting princesses and skeleton generals and blown straw and angry swans all hissing and aiming blows of their powerful wings all around them.

Ormestone in one of his wild sword swings clipped one of the swans, and Jacques tumbled suddenly out of the air. Jacques picked himself up and ran over to his father, who though he stood in manacles, hugged him. Then Jacques ran back furiously towards Ormestone, who raised the sword again and would have sliced Jacques in half if Jack had not earlier taken his bow from the cart. He aimed an arrow at Ormestone, hitting him on the sword arm, and the sword tumbled to the ground.

Ormestone rounded angrily on Big Jack Trueheart. He unlocked the manacles and then pulled out a sharp dagger from under his cloak. Jacques meanwhile fell and grabbed at the dropped sword.

'Move,' said Ormestone. He pushed Big Jack Trueheart over to the tall central tower of the Dark Castle away from all the fighting.

Jacques picked up the sword and struck out at the other four swan brothers, and as soon as the blade touched them the Trueheart brothers one by one tumbled out of the air. Jackie, Jackson, Jacquot, and Jake were soon all out of breath on the ground, still dressed in their tattered wedding clothes.

The princesses fought bravely and despatched skeleton soldiers one after the other. Jack finished the remaining ones with some well placed arrows. Soon enough the terrace was empty but for princess brides, Trueheart brothers, collapsed skeletons, and the whirl-wind strands of blown straw that had once been gold. The princesses fell into each of their Trueheart brother's arms.

Then Jack said shyly, 'Everyone, I'd like you to meet my Jill.' They all said hello to Jill.

Jill said, 'I was under a spell from that goblin and was cruelly changed into a carthorse, and now I am turned back into Jill.'

Jack looked around at the desolation on the castle terrace. 'Now, where's Ormestone and where's our father? That swine has taken him somewhere, and there's no sign of our Tom either.' Then they heard a sudden cry from the high tower. 'So that's where they are then. Look, he means to get away in that thing,' Jack shouted, and he looked up at the tower and the spiral stairs rising up among the dark clouds with the airship bobbing from the top.

Jack began to run across to the staircase. He looked up at the top of the high tower again, stopped and rummaged in his travel bag. He pulled out the strange cloth bundle and straps that the dark sprite had used to float to safety on the ground, and he strapped the whole thing on. 'I know it's damaged but it's worth a shot, it might still work, and better safe than sorry,' he said, and then he ran off and began to climb the high staircase.

At the last minute Jacques threw him the ceremonial sword, and as Jack caught it, Jill shouted after him, 'Be careful now, my Jack.'

Jollity the crow had spotted what Ormestone was up to. He saw him drag Big Jack Trueheart back to the castle tower. 'Come on, Tom,' and he flew like an arrow after Ormestone.

'Of course, he'll be going for the airship,' said Tom. 'Head for that.' They flew up high to the central tower, where the big black airship hovered ready for flight. Tom and Jollity landed on a high pinnacle and waited.

Sure enough Ormestone soon appeared, out of breath, and forcing Tom's father forward up the outside spiral of stone staircase.

'Dad,' Tom called out as they took off and flew towards them.

'Tom, my boy,' his father called back.

Ormestone turned in a fury, the knife still held close at Big Jack's throat. 'Oh, so it's you, is it,' he snarled. He dropped the dagger and quickly pushed Tom's father in through the airship's gondola cabin door and slammed it tight shut. Jollity aimed straight for him but Ormestone shook the crow away with blows and punches and with wild flailing of his arms. As soon as the bird was clear of his head Ormestone dived down again and picked up the dagger, which he had dropped on the steps.

At first the crow didn't realize what Ormestone was doing. He swooped down in a graceful glide with his wings outstretched. Ormestone got up quickly, in one fast move, and sliced at the bird with the silvery blade of his dagger. The crow felt a piercing pain, as if something white-hot had suddenly entered his chest. Tom fell off Jollity's back down on to the turret roof. Jollity tried to shout something out to Tom, but could only croak, just like a real crow. Finally after a huge effort the words 'Jollity hit,' slipped out as a croaky whisper. He could feel something wet dripping among his feathers. He was losing height. Ormestone got to his feet, laughing.

Tom picked himself up and hid for a moment behind a pinnacle. He saw Ormestone thunder past. He looked up and then saw the crow, good old, brave old Jollity the crow, coming to find him again. Tom dashed after the crow, hopping and skipping his way around all the details and features of the tall pinnacled roof, with its huge pointed fingers of stone. The crow was still flying but it seemed he was flying awkwardly now, that there was something wrong. Then Tom noticed a little blood was dripping from Jollity's feathers, down on to the stone work. Ormestone had stabbed or slashed the poor bird with the dagger. He was still waving it about, and from where Tom stood it was clear that Ormestone was going to kill the crow if nothing else.

'Here I am then, young Trueheart,' he shouted, 'as large as life and twice as ugly. Come and get me if you dare.'

He stepped forward, more menacing now, as the poor crow finally flopped down on to the stone not far from Tom, who stepped out from behind his pinnacle.

'Oh, there you are; such a little boy now. I see you've come to the rescue of your "familiar". Such nasty dirty birds crows, aren't they? They spend their time picking at bits of dead badgers and rats on the highways and byways, I believe. They call it carrion, ha ha.' He raised his arm up and wide suddenly and waved his fingers wildly. The poor crow fluttered up and stirred a little and then fell back on to the stone.

'See,' said Ormestone, 'what a good scarecrow I would make. I think now you understand how it feels to be so small and pathetic and helpless under an enchantment.'

'I'm not pathetic,' said Tom, angry and upset, close to tears.

'Oh, but I think you are.'

He stepped nearer to Tom, who raised his little sword straight at Ormestone.

'And I'm not helpless either,' said Tom.

'Have a care, my young apprentice, that little weapon might be dangerous.'

Jollity the crow flapped and then settled his wings, and moaned a little.

'I'm here, Jollity,' Tom said.

'Look at your poor friend. Why, he will soon be naught but carrion himself. You should tend him, little tiny Tom Trueheart, or should I say Tom Thumb, before it's too late and I feed him and you to my own hungry carrion crows.'

Ormestone raised his skinny arms and yelled something out, and part of the castle roof lifted like a black wave. The murder of crows and a thousand black bats rose into the air as one and headed up towards the tower.

Chapter 40

Halfway Up the Stairs

Jack climbed the stone staircase that spiralled round the tall tower. He still had one arrow left in his quiver, and he held the sword out in front of him in case he met any skeletons coming down the stairs, but they mostly seemed to have mysteriously slumped over and stopped back on the terrace. It was almost as if some puppet master had stopped them all suddenly in mid movement.

Above Jack, and climbing fast on the same steps in his tiny boots was that very same puppet master, none other than the lovesick sprite Rumpelstiltskin. His heart was full of vengeance against his own master, Ormestone, who must have told those beautiful princesses Rumpelstiltskin's name, and so destroyed his great chance of happiness for ever. He had to get to the airship before it was too late. He clattered up the stairs as fast as he could, his little bent twig of a wand held out in his hand.

He was surrounded in an instant by a screeching cloud of crows and leathery-winged bats. He pushed his head down and carried on battling through them, dodging claws and beaks; it was like a storm of birds. Ormestone was clearly desperate. He had taken Big Jack Trueheart with him because he had lost all that sprite gold, and he thought that Big Jack had finally solved the riddle of turning base metal into gold. Rumpelstiltskin, however, knew different.

He finally reached the pinnacle of the tower and there was Ormestone wielding a dagger, his white hair blowing in the cold wind, with crows and bats swirling all around him. The sprite pressed up against the dark stone of the tower and watched. The little boy Trueheart was on the sloping tiles of the pinnacle bent over the body of a crow.

'Jollity,' Tom said, 'Jollity.' The crow's eyes were closed and his breathing was shallow. Tom buried his ear in the warm feathers of the bird's chest. He could feel the thump of the bird's heart. Ormestone loomed above them enjoying every second of Tom's agony.

'Quite something to watch a dream die, eh, Tom? Quite something to see the very thing you love most destroyed? Now you know how I felt watching my beautiful gold blow away as worthless straw. Somehow you did that, and you will pay for it. To think that you have at last met your pathetic father, and now he's safely locked up in there. Soon he and I will be gone for ever where you cannot follow, especially without a little bird to fly on, huh?'

Tom tried to ignore his taunting. He had found the cut near Jollity's throat, a gash really, and he had laid his head near it and pressed his hands against it among the bloodied feathers.

'It's all right, Jollity, you'll be all right, I'm here,' he whispered, over and over. 'Don't die.' And his eyes welled up with tears.

'Oh, how sweet,' said Ormestone. 'The boy, the tiny little boy, loves his filthy crow bird. Well, well, time to put it out of its misery now, time to be merciful like any hunter to an injured bird, even with vermin like that.' Ormestone stepped one step closer to Tom and Jollity, who were both lying together on the pinnacle roof, and raised his dagger which glinted in the cold light.

Chapter 41

A sudden great shrieking noise came from above. 'Oh no, look up there,' said Rapunzel, and they all looked up as one and saw the great cloud of birds and bats lift off the roof and descend in their thousands on the tower. At once the remaining brothers, their princess brides, and Jack's Jill, all started up the spiral staircase.

They had not got far when part of the cloud of birds and bats descended among them. The bats hooked themselves into Rapunzel's hair, the birds pecked at the brothers, the girls slashed at the birds and bats with their swords and axes, black feathers flew in clouds.

'He's taken our father up there,' Jacquot called out.

'Come on, we can get through this.' Step by step they fought against the birds and the bats. The higher they got the more dangerous and narrow the steps and the further there was to fall. The steps were cold and slippery too, and each Trueheart and princess bride clutched on to the other as they climbed.

Chapter 42

Ormestone stood over Tom and Jollity as, small and defenceless, they lay beneath him, curled together on the roof of the highest pinnacle. The bird looked still, dead most likely; perhaps he wouldn't have to waste his own energy in removing its head with his dagger. The airship gondola bobbed close by and inside was his prize, the Trueheart father, who looked helplessly out of the gondola window. Well, he was finally capable of turning base metal into gold at least. Ormestone felt that he could easily manage the ship by himself.

'I hope you are wallowing in this unhappy ending of yours as much as I am, young Tom Trueheart?' he said with a grin.

Tom raised his tearful face and looked up at the dark figure of Ormestone.

'I think he is dead, my poor good friend Jollity. I can't hear his heart any more. Please help me,' said Tom.

'Can't hear you very well, my little lad,' said Ormestone. 'But if you want my opinion I think it would be kinder to let me finish your carrion friend now; my blade is sharp, he he.' Ormestone knelt down close to Tom and Jollity, and whispered angrily to Tom.

'My gold was changed into straw, my plans have been ruined, or so you might think. But I have your once-proud father locked up in my airship. Your father has a skill that I need. He can turn base metal into gold. He finally proved it to me after a long time trying. It was the saving of him. My sprite, the pathetic Rumpelstiltskin, may have failed me, but your father will not.'

Tom was hardly paying attention to Ormestone's words. He felt for his sword under his cloak. Ormestone had underestimated him once before. He stood up straight and pulled the sword from its scabbard. He felt the strength in his arm flow from the sword. A dazzling blaze of light shot from the tip of the sword, and Ormestone covered his eyes and took one step back. Rumpelstiltskin watched, hidden in the shadows.

Tom held the sword with both hands; he could feel the power surge in his arms. The light was like a beacon and crows and bats dived and swooped nearer to the light, and they swirled around and behind Ormestone like a protective cloak.

'An impressive trick, little Tom,' said Ormestone, turning to the door of the gondola. 'You know, sometimes discretion is the better part of valour.' He jumped up on to the highest point of the pinnacle and unhooked the anchor rope. The bats and birds rose with him, shadowing him, and then Ormestone jumped down, opened the gondola door, and quickly stepped inside. The airship bobbed where it was for a moment.

Tom sheathed the sword, knelt down beside Jollity and laid his ear on the bird's feathered breast. 'Oh, Jollity,' he said.

'Here, Tom,' said Jollity.

The bird struggled up on to its feet. Tom looked shocked. 'Jollity,' he said, 'you're all right.'

'I feel fine, Tom. I had a supply of some healing forest moss tucked under my wing. It's an old sprite cure. It takes a while to work and it weakened me a little, but not for long.'

The airship began to drift away from the tower.

'He's getting away,' said Tom, 'come on.'

The crows and bats flew around the airship like a cordon.

Tom climbed on to Jollity's back. Rumpelstiltskin

stepped out from the shadows. He looked over at Tom, pointed his little stick and there was a flash of light and sparks.

Jack blundered up the last few stairs, sword in hand, and Rumpelstiltskin turned to him and pointed the twisted little stick again.

Jollity flew up into the air and then there was a flash of sparks and then another. The crow shot upwards and then spun in the air; he had to flap his wings hard to stay level. He looked down at the pinnacle just in time to see Jack get hit with a bolt of sparks. Jack flew up in the air too, letting go of the sword.

Tom was thrown clear from the back of his friend Jollity and was suddenly back to his old full size again, and he just caught the sword with his free hand. Another flash and another bolt of sparks hit Jack and he blundered off the edge of the little roof, and, as he reached instinctively out for help, he gripped on to Tom, and they both fell from the high pinnacle wrapped in each other's arms.

The little sprite leapt up into the air himself and landed squarely on the back of the airship gondola. He clambered along on to the upper part and then disappeared from view under the shadow of the black balloon.

Jollity dived down towards Tom and Jack who were tumbling freely in the cold air. 'Follow the flying machine,' Tom shouted. 'Keep up with it, my old friend.'

Jack pulled the cord on his chest and the black cloth suddenly opened, and fluttered and flapped and billowed out above them. Although some of the strings were cut it broke their fall just enough, and they both drifted slowly down past the astonished princesses and the other Trueheart brothers until they landed on the remains of the gold, the huge pile of windblown straw, and rolled into a heap of arms and legs and swords and black cloths.

Jollity had watched as the cloth opened, and once he was sure that Tom was safely on the ground he headed back towards the airship and followed it.

In the gondola cabin Big Jack Trueheart was chained securely against a brace, while further off in the forward part, the stitched-faced man had set the controls for a new destination. Ormestone stood forward, looking out of the big window at the dark sky while his honour

guard of bats and crows flew around and alongside. The big black ship turned south away from the pinnacles of the Dark Castle. An extra passenger, the little sprite Rumpelstiltskin with his crown of leaves still on his head, crouched low and shivering on the gondola roof, biding his time, waiting.

Among the honour guard one crow bird in particular flew very close to the portholes of the gondola. He flew fast and felt full of fresh energy and renewed vigour, and by turning his head just a little he could keep an eye on Tom's father. He had no idea where this new story was taking him, but he could only hope that Tom would be a part of it, and soon.

Chapter 43

Tom had been awake since six o'clock. He was well prepared. The dreaded white velvet suit was freshly cleaned and pressed and waited like an omen of doom on a hanger in the wardrobe, and as far as Tom was concerned that was just where it was going to stay. He opened his window. It was a perfect summer morning, just right for the biggest wedding of the year. There would be six brides and six grooms now, for Jack would have his Jill and naught should go ill.

Tom opened his window and climbed out on to the sill. Then he shimmied down the drainpipe, cheerfully scuffing his breeches, and jumped quickly, lightly, down into the garden. He retrieved his packstaff, packed tightly with useful things, and his birthday sword from where he had hidden them the night before. The blade sparked just a little as he slipped it into the scabbard on his belt. He checked his Bureau maps and the confidential and secret letter which Cicero had left for him.

He felt excited at the thought of seeing his old friend Jollity again. He went out and stood in the middle of the garden and breathed in the good air of a summer morning in the Land of Stories, perhaps for the last time in a long while. He looked up at the weathervane of the house. A big glossy black crow sat perched there looking down at him.

'Is it really you, Jollity?'

'Yes, Tom, it is really me, come to rescue you from the pageboy suit as I once promised.'

The bird fluttered down and settled on Tom's shoulder.

'Right,' said Tom. 'Now that seems right again, you on my shoulder rather than me on yours. Off we go then, Jollity, before someone sees us. I've got a father to find and rescue.' Tom and the crow set off in the bright sunshine to walk to the crossroads.

Tom's mother quickly tucked the kitchen curtain back into place after Tom and Jollity had disappeared from view. 'That's my good boy,' she said. Then she opened the door and called up the stairs, 'Come on now, you lot, breakfast time. It's your wedding day, *again*, in case you didn't know it. Look lively.'

IAN BECK was born in Hove on the Sussex coast in 1947. After seeing an exhibition of drawings for the *Radio Times*, he was fired with enthusiasm about illustration and becoming an illustrator. He began attending Saturday morning painting classes at the nearby Brighton College of Art. Ian left school at fifteen and went immediately to Brighton to study art full-time. There he was taught by both Raymond Briggs and John Vernon Lord. He has since published over sixty books for children. One of Ian's titles, *Lost in the Snow*, was made into an animated film for TV, and his books have now sold over a million copies worldwide.

Visit Ian's website
www.tomtrueheart.com

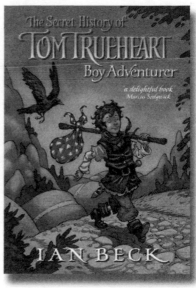

THE VALE of WOODCUTTERS

THE DARK CASTLE

THE LAND OF DARK STORIES